Irredeemable.

Chapter One-

    Angry obelisks of black smoke rose warily above the thin, desert hardy trees. Monuments left by the ragged excuse of an army that had recently pillaged the small village. One amongst a swath of ruined places now spoiling the landscape along the sea. This one, too small for a name of it's own, was near the walled city of Ma'arra. Well within two day's leisurely walking distance, even if you had only one good leg.
    A young faced man with dark, curling hair and brown eyes full of interest sniffed at the evening air from the relative obscurity provided by the thin line of trees. The smell of burnt flesh and spilled blood endured on the fading wind. His eyes flashed red for an instant, the aroma grinding at the edges of his appetite. He growled low in his throat. Urging himself to wait. Willing himself to be patient. Night would fall soon enough. Then his own small form would be harder to discern from the blackened backdrop of ruined houses.
    He crouched in the brush without moving. Without stretching, or flexing muscles. He could

wait. And wait. And wait. All muscle fatigue fading as soon as the sting blossomed. An attribute he had inherited from his long dead mother. One of the more welcome traits of many such which he bore.

The sun dipped in a firey haze over the low hills, where the man had spent countless evenings watching it pass beyond the sea to the west. The wind had picked up again and was blowing his scent toward the village now. A strange, impossible mixture of human and necrosis. A blend of two prolific races, he was the only one of his kind in all of existence. And he knew it deep in his core. The settling of aloneness was as heavy as wet ash in his stomach.

As the dark fell in full, his barely contained hunger began to demand attending. He rose from his place in the shadows to steal into the dead village. The almost moonless night, bright to his now burning red eyes. He didn't bother to check food stores, or search for missed loot. The village was poor enough to not have much of anything, and he personally had no use for either anyway. He cared very little for the currencies of humans. His sure path led towards the pile of half charcoaled corpses.

He closed his eyes and tilted his head slowly back. "Ah. They are all burned. Too bad. Too bad." He growled quiet and deep. A manic grin spread across his pale face, his teeth gleaming in the glow of the dying embers.

As he bent to his repast, the sound of bones splintering and now tough flesh tearing between his strong jaws broke the silence of the early night air. Tendons snapped. Layers of crispy fat were peeled from overcooked meat with glee. Swallowed down in exuberance. A look of sensual euphoria settled on his face. The intoxication of his desire to consume urged him on with eager impulse. He ate without pause until there was nothing remaining of the few people who had only hours before filled the village with life.

It was well into the night when he leaned against a smashed clay brick doorframe. Eyes closed, he sighed with contentment. He was still hungry. He was always hungry. But the desperation and urgency of his appetite had been stilled. Quieted. Mollified.

It had been too easy of late. Too simple to follow black smoke to a meal. Too many villages were being razed and pillaged. His human half frowned at the thought. In the same breath, his other, hungrier half was laughing with unbridled mirth. Death sustained him, after all.

He closed his eyes and inhaled deep and slow, to quiet the red. And to sooth his guilt at eating the bodies, instead of giving them proper burials. "I did not kill them. I could have. But I did not. I did not." He whispered, this time in Arabic.

When he finished consoling himself, he stood to leave, and was nearly surprised when he heard voices coming from the road a short distance away. The shuffle of unsure footsteps in the dust as loud to him as if he were making them himself. Instead of sneaking away into the night, he moved to the deep shadows of the broken house he had been reclining against. As quiet as death, he listened to the intruders converging on his hiding place.

"The desert take you, Yahir. You will see us both dead, chasing after hidden coins that were likely found or spent already." A male voice.

Young and spoken with a nasal whine. "It is not safe. Not at night. Not unarmed."

"Don't tell me you are still afraid of the desert demons!" The second voice was deeper, and chiding. He laughed, a short haughty huff of air. "Are you afraid of the Alghul, dear Seff? Will they come out to eat you without your mother's back to hide your ugly, frightened face?" A true laugh then.

"Shh! Will you be quiet?" Seff begged. "I am at least wary of the ones who have been doing this to the villages!" His voice dropped to a whisper. "Some may still be around, or may have returned with the same idea in mind as we have. And we have brought nothing with which to purchase our safety from them. My father says they may even come back later on to try their luck in Ma'arra again."

The man hiding in the dark bit back a distasteful growl. He knew these two. He would enjoy killing them to feed his void. But he enjoyed the passing company of most of his neighbors in Ma'arra too much to hide his guilt of their deaths. And he respected their families too much. Their families were kind people. Welcoming and friendly. These two, however, were not. They were conniving. They were self serving. They were petty thieves. And they were annoying.

But they would taste so gratifying. The man closed his eyes as they flashed red at the imagining of the last frantic twitches of muscle in his ardent teeth. The warm rush of blood down his throat towards his greedy stomach. "Ah." He nearly croned.

The sounds of Yahir and Seff rummaging around the house abutting his hiding place brought him back from his delirious fantasy. He took another calming breath.

"Something is wrong." Seff was always the nervous type. But now his voice cracked.

"Yeah." Yahir seemed to agree. "It's all gone. Those filthy, unwashed Christian bastards took it all. Even found the coins hidden in the bottom of the flax vase." He seethed the words as he spit.

"No, not that. Yahir, look around. Something else is missing."

"Everything is missing, you halfwit." A strong rebuke followed by what sounded like a cuff to the back of the head.

"I'm being serious!" Seff whispered as loudly as he could. "There are no bodies, Yahir! Where are the bodies?"

"Not more of your desert demon shit, Seff. I am sick of it tonight." But he didn't sound as confident as he had a moment before. All of the bluster sifting as sand from his boastful pride.

The man hiding in the shadows grinned with all the endearment of a madman. His brown eyes burned crimson with the wicked idea now forming in his mind. A low growl rumbled in his throat. Soft at first, then louder. He was speaking in his mother's tongue. The language of the Udughul. He called the humans by the equivalent of their names, knowing they would not understand.

"Yahir, Seff. You imbeciles are much too cumbersome for the night. You could be ingested if you are not more cautious." He growled loud enough for the rolling vibrations to reach their weak, human ears. The insult would sound only like an animal to them. Or at most, like the primitive language of his mother's people.

"Yahir, did you hear that?" Seff's teeth were rattling together and the smell of his fear was thickening in the darkness. "There is something in the next house. What should we do?"

There was the sound of rummaging through the remains of household items. "If it is a lion," Yahir whispered, his bravado returning, "I will hit it with this. You take up a shard of that pot by the door, and you can slice it's throat while it is distracted."

"What?!" Seff forgot to whisper. "There's no way that would ever work! The lion will kill me and I will be at the gates of Jahan'am waiting for you to arrive a moment later!"

"What if it isn't a lion? Will you fight it then? Or would you rather wait for it to come to you?" Yahir asked. "Come with me, or die here in the dark all alone." His footsteps made soft padding noises through the blackness, moving towards the door.

The man in hiding waited until the sound of Seff's own unsure footfalls fell in behind Yahir's. He moved with silence to the corner of the house which could be seen from its broken doorway and closed his burning, red eyes in joyful anticipation. The scent of the pair's fear was intoxicating. And enticing. And dangerous. He could lose himself, if he wasn't careful. He could take his prank too far. He forced himself to breathe, just as his unknowing victims peered into the darkness.

"There, see?" Yahir's voice shook. "Nothing."

Seff swallowed hard. "How can you tell? It is as black as the void inside."

Another growl made the two freeze in the doorframe. The man in the shadows let his mad grin spread wide across his pale face. When he opened his eyes to glow suddenly in the bleak cavern of the demolished house, he was delighted by the sight before him.

Yahir was petrified with fear, unable to move and had forgotten the makeshift weapon in his white-knuckle grip. Seff was screaming. Screaming and running into the moonlit night.

"Alghul! Alghul! Alghul!" He cried into the desert. Sadly, away from the path to Ma'arra. He would need to be herded in the correct direction, or he really would be eaten by lions before morning.

"Run home, human." The man with eyes the color of blood spoke in Arabic with a slight growl and a heavy accent, the way most humans thought an Alghul might speak. "Hide your ugly face behind your mother in fear of *desert demons*."

Yahir lost his bowels in his pants then. The smell of it filling the space between him and the monster. Finding his voice, he shrieked and stumbled over his own feet out of the ransacked village.

The man in the shadows laughed. A low and rumbling sound from deep in his chest. The laugh of an Udughul. The laugh of an Alghul. The laugh of a desert demon.

Chapter Two

"Amrit! Amrit!" The call came from the bend in the road a short way before one could actually see the tiny house at the end of the road no wider than a path.

"Amrit! Are you not awake yet? Have you heard?"

Amrit grinned as Nadav ran headlong into the low stone wall bordering his garden. It was the only way he could stop running once he got going. His left foot was slightly crippled from an injury during his childhood, and never quite worked the way he wanted it to.

"Have you heard?" The boy's gasping breaths made it difficult for him to continue as he made his lopsided way to his friend who was tending a vegetable patch. "Remember I told you Yahir and Seff were gone? That they had snuck out a few nights ago? They went to the south village the Christians burned to search for old Uzziel's secret coin box that he always bragged about in the market. Seff wound up wandering the desert all night chased by lions. Barely made it home, his sister says. Says it took a good slap to the face to make him talk in proper Arabic. He kept muttering about eyes chasing him and staring at the door like it would slam open at the slightest provocation. But Yahir, oh Yahir. He'd be having his hide tanned right now if he hadn't come in with his pants full of his own bowels!"

Amrit bent to pull a weed in a false attempt to hide his smile. He knew Nadav had already seen it. Was in fact, even expecting Amrit's quiet reaction. The sly amusement of the man who was as much a stranger as he was a friend in the city of Ma'arra as one could possibly be after living just at the outskirts, beyond the walls for nine years. "And what, if anything, had them so out of their minds to motivate such ludicrous behavior of two grown men?"

Nadav smiled with mischief. "You won't believe me. I could hardly trust my own ears when I heard it. Yahir, *Yahir* claimed there were desert demons! *Yahir*! Of all people!" His laugh was full of mirth. "I can hardly stand the irony of it, Amrit!"

Amrit allowed the youth time to finish his snickering before handing him a pair of baskets from one of the rows of his garden. "Since you are here, you can assist me." He filled the baskets to the brim with onions, asparagus, turnips and pears, and every other fruit and vegetable he had ready to harvest. He layered them carefully, placing the sturdier foods in the bottom to avoid bruising the softer fare.

"Aren't you even a little bit curious, Amrit?" Nadav asked as they worked the rows of the garden. "Desert demons, Amrit! I tell you that he says he saw Alghul, and you don't so much as scoff. I know you aren't from anywhere near here, and you probably think we're all bumpkins to still believe in man eating monsters wandering the sands. But it's Yahir, Amrit. My overbearing, practical, non believing brother, Yahir." He stopped moving down the row to pout at the man he thought only a few years his senior.

"What did they look like, these desert demons?" Amrit inquired to indulge the boy. "And how many were there?" He added before the first question could be answered. "Tell me how he knew they were truly Alghul, there in the dark, and not jackals, or leopards?"

Nadav smirked and leaned in close to whisper in a conspiratorial tone. "The eyes were pools of burning blood, Amrit. It was too dark to see anything else, but the eyes were bright and burning red. As if made of the embers of Jahan'am's own fire pits." He leaned back on his heels. "Ah! There hasn't been a sighting of an Alghul around Ma'arra for almost ten years now. I would very much like to see one. My brother is luckier than I am."

Amrit tilted his head to the side. "If what you say is true, then your brother is indeed fortuitous. Primarily to be alive. But he is also an idiot." He gave the tan skinned youth a half grin. "It may sound nice to be a lucky idiot, but I would not wish such tedium on you. Those two are always caught in some form of easily avoidable trouble."

"Bah, what do you know?" Nadav returned the smile. "You're not old enough to be wise."

He received a reprimand of a slap on the arm with a long bean and quiet laughter.

Nadav knew that few people in Ma'arra liked Amrit. They didn't like his pale skin, or his overly reserved behavior. They found fault in his lack of desire to eat the meat of animals, even fish, since it meant he was not buying any in the town. There were no rumors of clandestine nighttime meetings with women, or even men to gossip about, which led to other interesting stories. Nadav's own family believed the man to be a eunuch. The only thing most people really knew for certain, was that he wasn't from Ma'arra, and that was well more than enough to estrange him.

But Nadav enjoyed his company despite the man's oddness. Amrit was kind, and he was educated, and he was generous. He had successfully taught Nadav his numbers and writing when the tutors were failing. Had done so in a way that was easy to find engaging as a child. It was as if he were in no hurry for his student to master the lessons.

And Nadav also knew that most of the garden the man maintained was given away to the people in the most need of it. Namely the orphans and widows or the cripples in the slums. It was a wonder there was any left for Amrit by the time he finished passing it all out. But there must have been, because the man had yet to starve to death.

"Who's this for then?" He asked, hefting a basket to his shoulder. "You've gone heavy on the lentils and figs this time."

Amrit smiled warmly. "Ah, you noticed. The woman Hariel, who recently lost her husband on a trade ship. You remember the small wind storm we had a few weeks ago. It was a good deal more than rough on the sea. She has three children who are growing fast. And I have it on the highest authority that they love my figs the best."

"You've been sneaking into town to play with the children again, haven't you?" Nadav laughed to imagine it. It was not something a proper man would do. But it was the same way they had often met, when Amrit first came to the city.

Amrit's low, quiet laughter gave him away. "I am guilty of this, yes. Wait just a moment, and we can take these into town together."

Amrit vanished into his tiny house under the shade of his fruit trees. Many of which he had planted there himself. Where in the wilderness he'd dug them up from, only he knew. He returned a short time later with a shemagh so vibrantly red that it made Nadav think of blood, a color no one else in Ma'arra would wear as it gave no implications of political or regional ties. He wrapped the scarf around his head and face in the fashion of the desert dwellers to the south, and pulled a pair of sand goggles carved out of bone from a fold in his shirt. Nadav had once asked Amrit how much the goggles cost him and what kind of bone they were carved from, but had only received a wry smile in answer.

When he wore the sand goggles with his shemagh, none of Amrit's face was visible. The thin slit for each eye did not give away more than a darkened shadow beyond.

"You do realize that doesn't help people to like you, don't you? I have heard some of the merchants complain that you might rob them. If you have no truly good excuse, I might start to believe you actually are a bandit from the far deserts." Nadav always had the same line for his friend when they went into the city together. "It would make for an excellent tale." He raised his eyebrows as high as he could get them and made a point of looking his companion over as they made their way down the path.

"I could be, and you would not know it." Amrit tilted his head to the side. "Not until I have robbed you and run back to my compatriots in the sands carrying your vast wealth with me, that is."

"Oh, Amrit, I get that you are sensitive to the sun, with your pale skin it makes sense that you would burn. But, you really do look sinister." Nadav grinned.

"Ah," Amrit conceded, "I do not mind. The children think it is exciting when the heathen bandit comes to play with them. They have told me so much. Especially when I bring them pistachios."

"It's bribery, then, is it?"

"You have caught me yet again." Amrit shrugged. "Soon, I fear I shall have no secrets from you, dear Nadav."

They passed through the first gate of Ma'arra and made their way towards the ramshackle dwellings where the less prosperous members of the town lived crammed together with too little food, and too little room. The number of beggars and orphans continued to swell daily with the arrival of refugees in the wake of destruction left by the Christians from the north. Especially after their failed attempt at taking the city at the beginning of the summer, people swarmed to the safety of the walls.

Amrit walked as he always did in town, just a little closer to the buildings and away from the worst of the crowds. He stopped a few bold pickpockets from relieving Nadav of his purse and the food he carried. And even a few wandering hands from his own person. He did not have the habit of carrying any coin, but neither was he fond of being touched. He had trouble controlling his less civilized impulses when people were too close. His face was already stretched in an eager, manic grin beneath his shemagh. And his eyes were flashing red with his natural desire to consume. He had to concentrate simply to resist growling under his breath.

Nadav, of course, noticed none of this. His own preoccupation with their trek through the masses kept him busy with the basket in his arms. He chatted merrily, oblivious to the crowds and the heat, both growing with the ever rising sun.

"Don't you think so, Amrit?" Nadav had reached the end of a thought, but Amrit wasn't there to reply. Nadav looked around himself, mystified at the other man's ability to vanish. When he finally spotted his friend, he shook his head and clicked his tongue. "Amrit. I am beginning to think that you don't know the reason they always go straight to you."

"What?" Amrit shrugged as he handed another nearly emaciated beggar a handful of fresh greens. "I have more than enough. Besides, will anything I own follow me beyond the grave?"

Nadav's youthful laughter rose above the hum of the crowds. "I have my own religion, Amrit, you can keep yours! It's much too somber for my tastes. And far too altruistic. I do believe you are more patient than I."

Amrit sighed. "No man is perfect, Nadav. But I like to believe there may still be some small hope for my soul. That maybe I am not completely irredeemable."

By the time Amrit was finished passing out small portions of edibles to the beggars, Nadav's was the only basket left with anything in it. During this time, Nadav had slapped away a few of the more eager fingers from the basket in his charge, and heard the soft laughter of Amrit. "Of course, he thinks it amusing." Nadav grunted to himself as his friend swept away from the remaining stragglers.

"Amrit," the young man stepped in close. "I really am perplexed at how you can continually give away so much. I have seen you pick your garden bare for others, and yet you seem to have never gone hungry from it. You aren't buying fish from the vendors in secret, are you?"

"Ah, if you ever manage to unravel that particular detail of my life, I will give you my sand goggles. And I will ask nothing for them in return." Amrit left out the more gruesome details of what that discovery could entail. No good would come of it if the knowledge of his birth was spread. He had seen the heads of his mother's people lining some of the roads on the way to Ma'arra when he first arrived. And while there was no love between him and the maternal side of his family tree, he had no delusions that he would be treated any better than they were by the local people.

Tilting his head skyward, he breathed deep. The smell of the humans around him was strong in the mid morning sun. Pleasant. Enticing. Appetizing. Delicious.

Upon delivery of the remaining basket of produce, the newly widowed Hariel fell to the ground and wept her gratitude. Nadav poked fun at Amrit's discomfort when one of Hariel's older children suggested he would make a good substitute father and husband. They managed to peel themselves away after refusing even a drink of water from the already struggling household.

The pair found their way towards the fountain, where a large group of children could always be found playing and harassing the old men. One of the youngest spotted Amrit's red shemagh and shouted to the others who crowded around him eagerly, while Nadav found a seat at the edge of the well where he rested his tired left leg. There was some mild jostling for the closest position amongst the children, and a few of the smaller youths were pushed back.

Amrit shook his head and clicked his tongue. "What have I told you?"

"Sorry, Amrit." An older girl spoke up. "We are to care for those weaker or poorer than us, before ourselves."

The man swathed in red waited patiently for the crowd to shift around him again. He nodded once when they had finished. "Good. Just remember," he began to pull handfuls of roasted pistachios from the secret depths of his pockets, "I always have more than enough for everyone."

Squeals of joy and laughter erupted from the children.

"What game shall we play?" Amrit asked when all of his admirers had enough of the treat.

"Find us!" The vote was almost unanimous, and the children scampered off in different directions while Amrit turned his face skyward so the children would know he wasn't peeking through his goggles, and counted to one hundred.

Nadav remembered playing this game with Amrit, as well. He still didn't know how the man was so good at it. He never missed a child, no matter how well hidden they were.

Sure enough, this time as well, Amrit found every single one of them. The sound of his quiet laughter was warm when the children accused him of watching them hide.

Chapter Three -

The sound of dogs barking in the distance made Amrit pause. The early evening air was heavy around him with the lingering scent of his gruesome meal. He had come across the stringy man strangling a prostitute in a back alley and snapped his neck with a single strong, steady twist. Thankfully, the woman was unconscious from the now dead man's administrations. She would likely have a ring of purple around her neck for a while, but she was alive.

Amrit surreptitiously carried the body to an abandoned house with the roof caving in. He had only begun to attempt to sate his endless hunger when he heard the dogs. It wasn't the usual sounds of the dogs in the village. It was a distinct pattern of short barks. A pattern that he recognized. An irritated growl escaped his throat. It wouldn't take him long to finish his meal and move on, but he liked to pretend to have the option of taking his time. On the unlikely chance that his appetite suddenly became less voracious.

With a resigned shrug, he bent to his unholsome task. He needed to hurry anyway, he was expected at a dinner party.

A short time later, Amrit used the remains of the man's clothing to wipe himself clean of the evidence of his repast. He replaced his deep red shemagh and sand goggles. Slipping back into the fading light to rejoin the last of the crowds in the streets for the walk to his original destination. He made sure to pass close by the spice and perfume stalls, despite the way it burned his senses, hoping to mask the undertone of his not quite human scent from the equally sensitive noses of the dogs.

On the opposite side of town, Amrit removed his face coverings as he entered the spacious home of Nadav's family. One of the servants led him beyond the outer courtyard and into the dining area where the other few guests and family members had already begun to lounge on soft cushions around low tables.

"Amrit! You made it!" Nadav stood and showed his friend to a place beside his own.

"I would not miss such a joyous occasion. A birth in the family is meant to be shared. I am most honored to have been invited to the celebration for your new niece, Nadav. Your elder sister must be overjoyed. And I have brought her a gift." He bowed his head respectfully and placed a small, blue bowl with golden winged horses etched into the outer sides on the table in front of him.

"It's lovely, Amrit." Nadav's mother played her part as hostess by acknowledging the gift. "You are as generous as ever, it must have cost you a small fortune. It is a shame that the birth was so difficult for her that she is unable to join us, but praise Allah they are both well." She made a gesture of gratitude and instructed a male servant to display it in the main hall.

Amrit bowed his head slightly to the matron of the household. "No gift is enough to express how grateful I am for the friendship of your family." A servant came around to pour him a mildly fermented drink but he held up his hand and smiled. "No, thank you." The young girl lowered her head in silent acknowledgement and moved on down the tables.

Yahir huffed at the pale man. "The same as ever. You show up and speak pretty words, and sit so demurely at our tables. But you always refuse to drink our *nabidh*. I doubt you will even eat our food. I suspect the spiced foul will be too rich for your sensitive stomach, as well." He didn't even attempt to hide his enmity towards Amrit, letting his voice rise above the chatter.

"I do apologise." Amrit lowered his head in supplication. "I am aware that others often consider my eating habits to be inconsiderate, but I must insist that I not partake in company."

"That is enough, Yahir." Nadav and Yahir's father spoke in a rumbling baritone. "You know as well as the rest of us that Amrit's culture is more demanding than most."

"But Father," Yahir began.

Karam cut off his eldest son."I will not listen to you use rude words to insult the man while he is welcome under our roof. You are not to behave so unseemly at my table. You may leave, if you find it too difficult a task for you to be civil." He turned to his guest then. "I'm sorry for my son's conduct, everyone tells me that I was too soft with him in his youth."

Amrit smiled. "A father who loves his children is not a thing to lament, Karam. The son who does not grow to appreciate such love, however…" He left his comment with a deliberate open endedness. The heavy smell of spice rolling off Yahir as he took to his feet and exited the room was strong in Amrit's nose. "An amulet against Udughul?" He wondered to himself, taking care to avoid breathing too deeply, lest he sneeze and draw the young man's already angry attention.

"Oh!" Nadav exclaimed with glee, breaking the silence that had fallen. "I almost forgot, Amrit! I wanted to tell you something that I learned in the square today."

"What bit of mischief might that be, dear friend, to have you so enthusiastic?" Amrit's calm, half smile giving away his interest.

"Believe it or not, I have some small proof that the desert demons are not just tales of fancy." Nadav was too keen on his topic to see the apprehensive glancing between his parents, as he leaned in close to relate his findings. Yet, though Amrit feigned blindness toward the action, he did not miss the uneasiness of the pair. "There are hunters in Ma'arra. They came this morning, entering the gates along with the sun over the sands. Three of them all wrapped as tightly as you when you go out. They have with them twice as many dogs as they are in number, large, and trained in the scent of only one thing. Can you guess what it is that they hunt, Amrit?" The young man's eyes were wide with excitement. The sides of his face stretched in a childish grin.

"Are they perhaps, rat catchers?"

"No! Amrit, they hunt the Alghul!" Nadav rolled his eyes. "Why are you so stubborn with this? There are people who hunt and slay the heinous, unintelligent monsters for a living; people who impale their ugly heads at city gates, and along trade roads, and you joke about their existence."

Amrit firmly bit his tongue, his practiced smile glued in place. The insult had not been intended for him, he reminded himself. The young man had not meant to stab him in the heart with his words. He did not know any better. He did not know.

"Ah." He let out the breath he had caught himself holding. "I do not mean to belittle your findings, Nadav. But I do not think I am feeling well this evening. Perhaps I should have sent my congratulations in my place." He stood and thanked the hosts for including him in their celebration, begging them off when they offered to send him home with some of the meal to eat in private. Placating them with kind reasurances when they asked if his change of heart was due to their eldest son's childish behavior.

Nadav waved at him from the front gate, promising to regale him with all he had heard about the hunters of the desert demons when next they met. Summer was ending and a cool breeze hinting at a light rain blew over Amrit before he re-covered his face in his shemagh. As he rounded the first corner, his eyes flashed red in the deepening darkness.

"Ah." He growled soft in his throat as he added the sand goggles to his face. "That hurt, Nadav. That hurt. Such biting words you have unknowingly used against me, my friend. Such dreadful, venomous words."

The path to the mosque was only lightly populated at this time of night. A few devout Muslim worshipers and one or two Christians who had made the long journey south in pilgrimage, mostly gave the heavily wrapped man wide enough berth. But, one drunken man swayed directly into Amrit's path, his arm waving out at Amrit for an instant. Then he meandered through the small groups as if they were only imaginative wisps of fancy, and not solid people at all.

Amrit tilted his head to the side as he watched the seemingly inebriated man stumble away. The scent of alcohol and dust flitting on the eddies of air left a sort of strange perfume in his wake. There was something else there, as well.

In an attempt to catch the masked scent, Amrit breathed in deeply. And sneezed. He'd inhaled too much of the man's dusty scent, and his sensitive eyes were beginning to water with intolerance. He turned away from the drunk, back towards his path to the mosque, and stopped in his tracks.

A Pshdar dog was standing in the road. The large hound had it's head lowered and tail still. The only movement it made was the rhythmic expansion of it's massive chest as it breathed. Amrit was glad that he was downwind from the beast. It would help to slow the animal from discovering his scent. The short barks of another Pshdar a short distance behind him dropped his throat into his stomach, and he growled a curse.

The drunkard. He had been deliberately touching people to get their scents for his dogs. And now they had *his* scent and he was caught in the middle of their tightening net. "Ah." He chastised himself. "I know better."

The dog in front of him raised its hackles and began to growl menacingly. The bark of the other dog had set it on alert, but it did not yet know which of the people walking along the road was the intended target. Amrit grinned like a madman under his shemagh, and darted to the left just as the wind changed. He leapt over a short wall and a stack of earthen jars before running down a narrow alley. The sound of baying behind him grew loud as the dog he had left behind recognized it's quarry.

When another large hound of the same breed appeared at the end of the alley, Amrit pushed off his left foot to bound up the wall to his right. His bare feet making muffled sounds on the sun baked clay and stone. He found himself on a flat veranda and cut straight across the rooftops to the east, toward the mosque.

A shrill whistle cut through the night and the dogs fell silent.

"Oh, good." Amrit thought. "A silent chase. So much more exciting." He loosened his shemagh and removed his sand goggles. The burning blood red of his eyes glowing vibrant in the cloud enhanced darkness. He laughed aloud. A cross between the deep rumbling of an Udughul's laughter and the higher, smoother laughter of a human. The thrill of the hunt shivered through him as he leapt across a road to another rooftop.

The rounded minaret of the great mosque rose pale against the rapidly cooling backdrop of sky. It was only a moment before Amrit was dropping into the courtyard and walking towards the inner square. He snagged an incense vessel from a niche carved into the wall. His eyes watered as he rubbed the overwhelming scent over his body before taking a place on one of the many colorful rugs laid out for prayer.

The strong incense made it near impossible to make out any other smells around him, so he relied on his ears instead. The sound of padded feet, and snuffling emanated from outside the doorway. The dogs had arrived. Then, Amrit heard the quiet voices of their masters.

"It can't have gone inside. It would burn to walk on such holy ground." One voice insisted, nearly causing Amrit to laugh at the misconception.

"It must have gone over." A second, older voice. "We'll send four dogs around. Maybe we can head it off. Rayyan, you will remain here in case it doubles back. Stay alert boy, this one is quick. And they're never alone."

"Yes, Zale." The rough voice replied with obedience and the sound of footsteps could be heard hurrying away.

Amrit waited a few minutes before saying a small prayer for the man he had killed earlier, and rising to his feet to leave. He forced the excitement to leave his smile, and the red from his eyes. A trick his mother's people could not perform, their eyes eternally burning embers in their madness stretched faces. He was eternally appreciative that he was half human.

It had begun to rain by the time he stepped back into the courtyard, washing away the lingering traces of his smell from the area. He stopped in the archway where the hunter called Rayyan was sheltering from the light, but steady shower. The human's scent condensing in the partially enclosed space.

"Curious." He thought. "You are not a man at all."

Out loud, he said, "Hello, mind if I join you in your alcove from the rain?"

"Oh," Rayyan turned around, surprised. "I didn't hear you approaching." The woman dressed as a man moved over to make room for Amrit before turning back to the task of watching for Alghul. "No. I don't mind at all."

"It is a nice night to be dry at home! I was hoping the rain would hold off until I reached mine, but..." he gestured to the wetness. "Are you waiting for someone this far into the night?" Amrit asked. "I saw you looking about as though they might be late in arriving."

"Not exactly," Rayyan squinted in the gloom. "I'm sorry, Mr..."

"Amrit. Just Amrit."

"Mr. Amrit, I'm actually a bit busy and I am afraid I do not have the luxury of engaging in polite conversation at the moment."

"Ah." Amrit tilted his head downward. "How impolite of me. It is a bad habit of mine, to strike up conversations with strangers, and you reminded me of someone. I will be on my way." He stepped out into the rain to leave.

"Mr. Amrit!" Rayyan nearly stammered. "It isn't safe out this night. Please see that you head directly home." Then as if just considering it would be wise to disclose the nature of the danger, "There are man-eating beasts about."

Amrit smiled warmly. He caught a glimpse of a softening around her eyes as he bowed his head graciously. "I will. Thank you."

The two remaining Pshdar hounds twitched their ears from the deep shadows as Amrit passed through the rain not more than twenty paces away, but made no other indication of interest. They were failing to catch his scent in the rain.

Leaving the mosque behind as the dwindling precipitation began to evaporate, he scaled the walls surrounding the city a short distance off. When he came closer to his small house framed by it's bountiful garden, he laughed with the mirth of a child playing pranks on the old men in the village square.

Chapter Four -

"Are you certain this is a good idea?" Seff was as nervous as a hen with new chicks. Looking about himself as if expecting some monster to leap out of the shadows. "These people are cursed, you shouldn't have sent for them in the first place."

Yahir rolled his eyes. "Oh, would you just shut up? We know what we saw out there. And *I* know what *I* saw leaving my house the night of my sister's celebration. There is only one in all of Ma'arra who wears that shade of shemagh, and a *human* does not have eyes that glow as embers in the night. Do you really think that monster will let either of us live once it catches on that we know?" He spit into the dust. "Because it won't. And I won't sit back and wait for it to come to me with it's slavering jaws and evil eyes."

"And you should not be asked to." A tall man wrapped tightly in a white shemagh stepped into the alley, followed by two more men dressed similarly. The first figure bowed his head slightly. "I believe I remember instructing you to remain home as much as possible,

Master Yahir, Master Seff. I do hope you have at least remembered to keep your amulets about your person and refilled with fresh Ras El Hanout at each evening, when the ghùl are most active."

Yahir sneered at the three hunters. "Your *magic* holds no sway over the beast, Zale. It *sat* at my table. It *conversed* with my *father*." His face heated with the stinging memory of the embarrassment of the evening of the dinner party. But he quickly paled with the memory of the blood red eyes outside his home as the one called Amrit went on his way. "It has fooled everyone. Everyone but me."

"That is not possible." The leader of the hunt replied. "If it is truly one of the ghùl, as you claim, it would not be able to hold it's deception under scrutiny. And to be so brazen as to enter your home where it would be alone and outnumbered, no ghùl would be so fearless as to place itself in such an unfavorable situation."

Yahir smirked then. "And yet, here we are!" He threw his hands out and spun around once with dramatic flair. "In an alley, discussing impossibilities while I have seen with my own two eyes the truth of it. It is not a man. It is a monster." Yahir stepped right up to Zale, glaring up into his eyes. "I know who it is, and I am paying you to put its disgusting head on a pike outside the city gates."

A sudden low growl erupted behind Yahir, and he heard Seff whimper. One of the giant Pshdar dogs was there, ready to protect it's master.

Zale swept away Yahir's raised hand from his view and signaled to the hound to sit. "I am in charge of this hunt. You may be providing funds, but I will have you understand that I would destroy the ghùl even without your payment. The added care for your personal safety is what you are paying for."

He looked down his nose at the shorter male, strongly punctuating his words as he did. "Our formidable knowledge of the demons is what you are paying for. Our extensive experience in the field is what you are paying for. Our capability and desire to exterminate the beasts, we always offer free of charge." He turned to leave the alley, signalling his dog to follow him as he did. "Stay out of our way. Let us do our job, and we will be sure to finish it properly."

Zale paused at the mouth of the alley. "Rayyan, get the new information from Master Yahir. I will leave it up to you to investigate the validity of his claims. We cannot go about killing people on fear and rumor alone."

"Yes, Master Zale." Rayyan's head remained bowed until the other two had gone.

When Rayyan turned intense brown eyes on Yahir, the man huffed indignantly. "You seem familiar, for some reason. I don't like it. Who is your family?"

"I have no family." Rayyan's reply was emotionless. "The ghùl dragging people away in the sands is my earliest memory. Tell me about your desert demon, or go home."

"This can't be right." Rayyan muttered to herself and signaled her two dogs to heel. She was closing in on the place Yahir had directed her to, but she was perplexed. It was just a house. Not a run down, abandoned hovel like the ones ghùl usually hid in. It was a normal, well kept house. The garden all around it was a bit odd and the number and variety of trees was certainly unexpected, but it was nice. And it was flourishing. Ghùl did not tend crops. They were strictly carnivorous. So, this simply couldn't be the place Yahir had meant.

"Hello." The voice startled her from her thoughts. She hadn't even noticed the man leaning against the inner corner of the short wall. His pale skin was striking in the shade of the date tree. "Nice day for a walk."

"Pardon my intrusion." Rayyan inclined her head briefly. "I was looking for someone. I am a visitor to Ma'arra, and was given the information in town that there is a man who grows pistachios, living beyond the walls. I am not certain if I have found the right place."

The man tilted his head to the side. "You might have. I do grow them, though I do not know why anyone would recommend mine."

Rayyan ran through the information Yahir had shared with her looking for a plausible story. "Children might."

The pale man smiled warmly then. "Ah, yes. They might." He straightened from his reclined position. "May I offer you a drink? The sun is bright and strong at the end of summer. Though, I have only water. And possibly some of my pistachios?"

"That would be most welcome, thank you."

The man stopped at the edge of the shadows and looked at Rayyan's dogs uneasily. "Ah, they are rather large. I am sorry, I have had some bad experiences with dogs and I am ashamed to admit I am still wary of them."

Rayyan nodded her head. "I understand, I have a similar dislike of the thing which once attacked me, as well. They are well trained, they'll stay here if I tell them to." She held out her hand in the sign for stay, and the dogs laid down in the path.

"Thank you. Let me retrieve that drink for you." The man vanished into his house and returned a moment later with a wooden cup filled to the brim with water, stopping at the short wall. "It is only a little, but it is fresh and cool." Rayyan loosened her face coverings just enough to expose her mouth. While she drank the water from the cup and handed it back, Amrit noticed the faded edges of scars under the white cloth.

As his guest straightened her shemagh, Amrit set the cup casually on the low wall and walked to the other side of his garden. He leaned over a box in the shade next to his house, humming quietly. He spent a moment choosing the best pistachios, picking out the less desirable ones. He sniffed at them carefully, looking them over in his hands before dropping a handful into a small, hand sized basket." He smiled as he held it out for his guest.

"Thank you. Please forgive my rudeness, I am Rayyan." She inclined her head in a polite gesture.

"Ah, yes. We have met, though I did not ask your name that night in the rain, Rayyan. You may not remember me from such a short meeting, I am Amrit." He held out a hand to implicate his garden. "Care to enjoy the shade while you finish your pistachios?"

"Mister Amrit?" Rayyan's eyes twitched in a moderate smile and she stepped into the walled space of Amrit's garden. "I was concerned you might not have made it home that night. "I am relieved that you did. I had my dogs with me when we first met, you must not have seen them or you might have avoided me altogether. It was rather dark, I recall."

Amrit laughed. A low and quiet sound. "I confess, I would not have made it past the exit without some duress had they been under the archway next to you." He resumed his own reclining in the shade as Rayyan made herself comfortable. "You said you are a visitor to Ma'arra. Is your family merchants, perhaps?"

"No, I am a hunter. I travel with two others, and our Pshdar's, of course." She shelled one of the roasted pistachios and closed her eyes for a brief moment after placing it in her mouth. "This is the sweetest pistachio I have ever eaten."

"That might explain why the children hold them in such high regards."

Amrit's childish grin at the compliment made Rayyan's cheeks flush. "Oh, Allah. What is wrong with me? He will discover I am not a man. Hopefully he will only think me *latah*." She thought to herself. Then to Amrit, "You did not happen to run into anything out of the ordinary on your way home that night, did you?"

Amrit shrugged his shoulders. "Nothing more out of the ordinary than a young man standing in the rain late at night. Was that man eating beast you spoke of the thing you are here to hunt?"

"Yes." She replied. "My band was hired to hunt a ghùl which was seen in the area. And we have reason to believe it may even be within the walls of Ma'arra."

"That is odd. I have never heard of one of their kind being so brazen. I have always heard that they are supposed to be cowardly and conniving creatures. Are you certain it is not some other form of demon, or a spirit, perhaps?"

"It is very unusual behavior." Rayyan agreed, nodding. "But our client verified the bright, blood-red eyes of the beast. He heard the growling speech of their kind, as well."

"Speech?" Intrigued by the not entirely derogatory way his guest remarked on the Udughul, Amrit tilted his head to the side. "The general consensus claims they are not capable of truly speaking."

Rayyan glanced about briefly. "Most people don't realize it, but that growling sound they make is a form of communication only a little different from human language. They can even mimic us. That's how they trick people into following them into the desert, where they can be more easily overcome and eaten."

"Ah, I see. That does make sense, otherwise why would anyone willingly chase them into their trap?" Amrit nodded amicably.

"They are far more clever than they're given credit for. Which is why it isn't uncommon for hunters such as my group to be hired for even just a single sighting. But wherever there is one, you can be sure there are more. They never travel completely alone unless they are purposely separated from their group by experienced hunters." Rayyan knew she was sharing more than she should, but Amrit seemed genuinely interested in her knowledge on the subject. And she was passionate about her trade.

"Is it true then, that they subside solely on human flesh? And that they must be killed in a single blow lest they revive with a second strike?" Amrit prodded. "Or that they are capable of predicting the weather, or drought? I am somewhat interested in your answers, you see. I would like to sift through the rumors for whatever truth you possess."

Rayyan laughed. "Oh, Allah! Only that first one is even near the truth. If they revived from a second blow, we would never be rid of the devils. And I know nothing of their ability to forsee anything of the future, unless they can smell the change in weather on the wind." She ate the last of her pistachios, meticulously replacing the shells in the small basket. "I have seen them eat small rodents, snakes, or even insects on occasion. But it never seemed to be particularly satisfying for them. It was only the truly emaciated ones who would partake in such fare."

"You do not speak as though you are so entirely disgusted by them, the way everyone else is."

"Do not misunderstand." Rayyan shook her head. "I wish to see them dead. Down to the very last, not even sparing the young. I simply believe that they are more like humans than we care to admit. And I feel that it is dangerous to underestimate even the weakest amongst them."

Amrit turned his face to the wind, silent for a moment. Then he smiled politely, rising to his feet. "I have enjoyed your brief company, I have too few visitors out here. But, I nearly forgot that I have a previous engagement to attend to, and the day will stand still for none."

"I almost overstayed myself, anyway." Rayyan stood and readjusted her face coverings once more, inclining her head as she did. "Thank you again for the respite in your shade and for the pistachios that were definitely worth the walk."

"Ah, before you go." Amrit strode to his box and filled three small cloth pouches, handing them to Rayyan. "One for each of your companions, and one more for you." He said with an almost devilish grin.

She thanked him again and walked back towards her dogs in the path. When she turned to bid Amrit farewell, he was nowhere to be seen.

"Strange." She murmured. The breeze shifted, gently sweeping over her from the now empty garden and she heard the low warning growl of her dogs erupt from behind her.

She glanced at her dogs, then in the direction of their intense gazes back towards the garden. She started to sweat then. Signaling the Pshdars to heel, she quickly made her way back to the city gates. This was more than she felt comfortable handling alone.

She would need to report to Zale and Marin what little she knew.

But, was Amrit a man? Or a monster? Or something else entirely? And what line made the definition? As she left the small house and garden behind, the light wind made a sound not unlike the demented laughter of a ghùl.

Chapter Five-

"Are you really leaving now, Amrit?" Nadav was leaning on the doorframe to his family's home. He rubbed his gimpy left leg with unconcious worry. "It isn't the safest time for travel."

Amrit sighed. "Ah. I know, I know. But something has come up and I find I really must leave for a while." He tried to smile at his friend. He had no desire to leave Ma'arra yet, but he had not even been back to his little house since the visit from Rayyan and her Pshdar hounds. He had left just in time to avoid the shifting of the wind. But there was nothing he could do about his lingering scent laying over the garden, and he knew the dogs had noticed.

"Your concern for my well-being is truly appreciated, Nadav." He bowed his head slightly. "I will return as soon as my business is completed."

"Fine." Nadav pouted. "Just make sure you have something with which to pay off the Christians, in case you meet with them unexpectedly. I would hate to receive word a

year from now that your worthless carcass was found rotting away in the desert, stripped of all worldly possessions."

Amrit's quiet laughter served to fill the short distance between the two. "I will. And if I find I do not have enough to secure my safety, I will bury myself in the sands until they have passed. Tell your mother I am grateful for the skin of water. I will save it for an emergency, God forbid I meet with one."

He turned to leave, pausing as he did. "One last thing before I go, dear friend. I have been meaning to tell you something for a while now, and I am concerned that I may not have another opportunity for quite some time." Stepping in close to Nadav, he whispered in the youth's ear. "It was not a dream, that long ago day in the sands. You truly were kidnapped along with your twin sister, who now lives in the guise of a man."

"What?" Nadav was startled. But Amrit only waved and smiled as he exited the courtyard, covering his face as he went.

What was that supposed to mean? And how did Amrit know about that dream? He had never before spoken to anyone but his parents about that. He furrowed his brow in thought. "Not a dream?" He murmured, his eyes growing wide. "All of it? Even the part with the gleaming red eyes and the blood stained sand?"

Nadav's head was too full to think clearly. There was no way it could be true.

He stalled a servant to send word to his mother that he would be walking about the market. He was in desperate need of a distraction, and the Alghul hunters were still in town. With any luck, he'd have a glimpse of them with their giant hounds.

He decided to visit the stalls and shops that Amrit would never go near. The perfume shops were closed off from the burning afternoon sun, but the heavy, overwhelming scents were enough to make his stay short in any of them. The headache that was blossoming between his brows made him respect his friend's sensitivity even more.

After Nadav had had his fill of perfume shops, he bought a skewer of roasted goat from a vendor and found a spot in the shade to rest his tired left leg. He plopped himself down right next to a spice stall and enjoyed the mixture of smells filling the space around him.

He was in the middle of rubbing the stiffness out of his calf, when one of the Alghul hunters appeared at the spice stall he was sat next to. As far as Nadav could guess, the hunter was the same age as him under all his layers. Only his oddly familiar eyes were left without some bit of cloth. While Nadav was immersed in trying to figure out why the stranger seemed like someone he should know, a deep *whoof* of air blew across his right cheek. Toppling over from the sudden fright, the unmanly squeak he was unable to contain caught the attention of everyone within earshot.

Everyone including the hunter he had been staring at. "Are you well?" The voice was rough as if affected by some old injury, but it was not unkind.

Nadav looked up into the deep brown eyes of the man holding out his hand to offer assistance. They were even more nostalgic up close. "Uh, sorry. Yes." He took the hand that was being offered and managed to right himself. "I was surprised."

"I was as well." The hunter admitted, petting one of his two large hounds on top of it's massive head. "The only human she normally gets that close to is me." He furrowed his brows a little. "You are the younger brother of Yahir, are you not?"

"I am Nadav. Do you know my brother?"

The hunter looked away briefly. "I have met him." He stepped back up to the spice stall to pay the vendor for a small leather pouch. "I am Rayyan. Come." He said to Nadav. "I will buy you a drink to make up for my dog's behavior." He waved over his shoulder and passed into the crowds.

Nadav had a hard time keeping up with the long stride of the hunter as he strolled with purpose down the busy street. "Hold on, please." Nadav gasped as he finally caught up, smiling weakly. "I have a bad leg, and I'm not used to walking with others. I usually only walk with Amrit, but I just realized that I never have to worry about his pace. Somehow he's always right beside me, no matter how bad a day I'm having."

Rayyan turned abruptly to face Nadav. "Amrit?" It was not a common name, there were few here who spoke Greek, after all. It couldn't be a coincidence. "Not tall? Pale? Speaks like an overly old man, yes? You know him?"

Nadav grinned mischievously. "You forgot quiet, and surprisingly quick. But most of all, cunning. I do. I am glad to call him my friend, despite his religious zeal."

Rayyan grabbed Nadav gently by the elbow. "I think I shall have to buy you an entire meal, Nadav. I am interested in your stories of this man called Amrit."

Amrit walked about the camp of the Christians without concern. He had traded his clothes for a set stolen from the corpse of an unwary guard, tucking his sand goggles in one of the pockets of the tunic. Plus, the night was dark, and he had already learned two of the languages they spoke amongst themselves a week ago. Rayyan was only partially correct on that point. The Udughul didn't mimic human language. They absorbed it. It was a very useful skill to possess when one wanted to blend in.

Amrit gave himself a silent reprimand for giving in to his curiosity. But, the ragged army was awfully close to Ma'arra again. Pieces of quiet conversation led him to believe that the Christians were dissatisfied with their trek to

Jerusalem. That they were starving. And that more than some of them might be feeling desperate.

He located a tent which seemed a degree more opulent than the surrounding shelters and made his way towards the light of the fire outside its entrance. Skirting around the shadows cast by the glowing flames, he settled himself in as though sleeping, leaning on a half broken cart. He closed his eyes and focused his sensitive hearing on the voices inside the tent.

"...know it was a complete failure with the walled city. But Pilet wasn't expecting there to be such fierce resistance. I feel very strongly that we can overcome them, if only we use a different tactic. If we can manage to distract them while the knights sneak in, we will have Marre, and we will have all of the spoils. You must admit that we are starving, Raymond. Besides, think of the riches they must be hoarding. We could be kings, you and I."

A tired sigh from the tent punctuated the darkness. "Bohemond, we are on a holy crusade. I care not for the riches, only for the conquest of the holy lands from the hands of these barbaric people. However, I do see the need for fresh provisions. Our men are wasting away since we lost our supply lines."

A moment of silence, then, "Alright. We will return to the north. Keep in mind, though, if we are unable to seize the city of Marre, we will be forced to find another way to feed our troops and followers lest they all die or decamp."

"Oh, lovely." Amrit grumbled to the sky. "You fiercely wish me back in Ma'arra, I see." After a stumbling soldier had passed by to relieve his bladder behind another cart, Amrit slipped out of the camp. "Fine. Hold my conscience and the weight of my soul over me." He growled a string of curses in his throat and turned himself northward, whispering a prayer under the star studded night.

Amrit's eyes flashed crimson behind his sand goggles. The small outcropping of rocks he had found was saturated in the scent of Udughul. There were multiple indentations in the dust indicating sleeping spaces and a few scraps of leather and cloth scattered about. Remnants of past meals.

"Hell." He murmured. He would have to kill them now. His scent was all over the place. He didn't specifically have anything against these particular members of his mother's race, but then again, every Udughul he had ever met wanted him dead. More than that. They seethed and fumed with their desire to tear him limb from limb. To consume the outcast. The *ghren*. The *half breed*.

It likely didn't help that he tended to attack them on sight, as well. Even after so many years, the anger still boiled over in him. It didn't matter that the ones who had killed his parents died on that same day. Until they were *all* dead, he knew he wouldn't be free of them.

Grinning like a mad man, Amrit left the outcropping far behind him. The trail of his mother's people was easy to follow. The smell of necrosis lingering behind them like a line of torches, guiding him through the coming dawn. It was only just after the sun was fully above the horizon that he saw his quarry in the distance. There were six of them and they were gathered around something, or someone Amrit could not see. The wind blew in fitful gusts from the west, sending his scent in horizontal lines away from the others. And it did not seem as though it would change within the hour.

It was an easy thing to creep up on them, as preoccupied as they were. The six were trying to decide if they should risk eating the obviously poisoned corpse they had found. Even with their naturally extraordinary healing abilities, depending on the poison and the dose, they could still die. Or at least suffer horribly. Stashing his sand goggles in a pocket, he moved towards the group.

"It would be unwise of you to eat it." Amrit growled the advice once he had snuck in close enough to startle the smallest female. "None of you would last the rising morning."

"And how can you tell? Oh, wise one." The leader of the group stepped up, growling at the newcomer. Six to one was considered acceptable odds with the Udughul, and it left them feeling confident.

Amrit made a show of sniffing the air, maintaining the short distance between them as he spoke. As soon as he was close enough to smell, there would be little time for discourse. "I know this, because I have experienced the effects of that peculiar poison before. I know that it will leave you retching violently for many hours."

The group laughed at that. "Then we shall be fine. It is unlikely that we would die of *vomiting*, brother."

"I should think not." Amrit's teeth showed white in the chasm of his grin. "But it would serve to keep you occupied during a physical encounter of the violent sort."

The female closest to Amrit sniffed the air and furrowed her brow. Tilting her head to the side she sniffed again. "His scent is wrong." Her burning red eyes opened wide as the realization of what she was smelling hit her. "It is the *ghren*!" The last and only words she was able to shriek before Amrit bit onto her tender neck. Snapping it with the force of his jaws.

"Ah." He sighed as the last twitches of muscle gave way to death between his teeth. A wellspring of blood surging from the wound coated him in red. A small shudder passed through Amrit as he swallowed the bite of flesh he had removed. "You taste horrible, but I am hungry. You will do to sate me, *cousins*."

He had dropped the corpse at his feet and was grabbing the outstretched arm a second

Udughul was aiming at his face, when two giant blurs of fur and fangs flew into his view, attacking the center of the group.

"Pshdars." Amrit growled and broke the arm in his hands. The wails of the Udughul were cut short when Amrit tore his stomach out with his strong fingers, letting the entrails gather like snakes in the dust.

A third dog leapt at him then, catching him on the shoulder with long fangs. Amrit grunted as the weight of the massive hound pushed him backwards to the ground, sharp claws tearing his stolen tunic and digging into his stomach. Growling with pain and irritation, Amrit used his legs to push the dog off of him. He rolled to a low crouching position and snarled at the animal. The wounds it had given him were already healing, but he was irked that his hunt had been interrupted.

"Where is your master?" He asked the beast in Arabic.

In answer, the Pshdar lunged at Amrit again. This time, Amrit caught it by the muzzle and used his own inhuman strength and the momentum of the dog's attack to rip it's lower jaw off in one violent motion. He was turning to face what remained of the brawl when a heavy net was cast over him. It was cold against his skin. "Iron?" He thought, smelling the metal. A deep rumbling laugh erupted out of him.

Two hunters came into view and he addressed them in Arabic. "You seem to be well prepared, *alsayadin*." They were not the ones hired to find him in Ma'arra. This was a group of two stocky men with overgrown beards. "And I see you graciously allowed one of them to get away. Trying to follow her to a den? It might not work. She was clever enough to run early."

He was kicked in the head and the bottom of the iron net was cinched shut around him. "Shut up." A deep voice from behind. "This one got Ams. I haven't ever seen one rip apart a Pshdar like that."

"What do you think, Esmail?" The one in front of Amrit crouched down to examine their captive. He laid his heavy, curved sword across his knees. "Do we really need two? The runner should be enough, shouldn't it?"

"We're down a dog, I don't see any reason to keep this one. More trouble than it's worth, right Nur?"

The one called Nur nodded once. "No reason." He stood and used his weight to pierce Amrit in the chest, aiming between the iron reinforced netting. Pressing hard into him to make sure the blade went deep.

Amrit cried out with the pain, growling obscenities when Nur pulled his now bloodied sword out for another try. "Get it's heart, Nur. Or the bastard will take longer to die." Esmail offered his unsolicited advice over their captive's wild, vocal complaints regarding his suffering.

"I did!" Nur's face twisted with frustration. "Both times."

"Let me try." Esmail added his own blade to Amrit's chest and was genuinely surprised to see that the wound began healing while the weapon was still embedded in the flesh. "What is this thing?"

Amrit cried out again as the blade was torn from him, his eyes burning furious blood red. "Ah! Foul blackened hell, stop it! If you cannot execute me properly, at least allow me to eat the Udughul I killed. Or I fear I may lose myself and eat you instead."

Esmail stood back, blinking and uncertain for a moment. Then he burst into laughter. "Ha! Do you hear this one? I have never in all my years in the hunt had one ask for a meal after failing to die!' Then he crouched down in front of Amrit and looked him in the eyes. "Why won't you die, ghùl? What magic are you using? Satisfy my curiosity, and I will give you all four of the dead to sate your hunger. I will even throw in the poisoned human corpse and the dog you killed if you answer well enough."

"Esmail, not Ams!" Nur protested and was hushed with his comrade's raised hand.

"I do not need the hound." Amrit conceded. "It is unfortunate, but I cannot eat it." His grin became malicious for an instant. "The Udughul, however, would be most gratifying to consume."

"Then speak, beast. Appease me with your answer to my question." Esmail's left eyebrow twitched upward with curiosity.

Amrit closed his eyes and inhaled the scent of the humans and the smell of blood and death, rumbling in his throat his desire to consume. "It is no magic which keeps me alive, hunter. It is a curse. The same one placed upon my father by God himself at the beginning of man's accounting of time. And it is the curse of my mother's blood running through me."

"What do you mean, ghùl? Explain in a way that makes sense, or I will continue with attempting to kill you." Esmail said with impatience, the tip of his sword held toward Amrit's stomach.

The hunter was met with the wide, excited eyes of the pale monster in his net. "Do you wish to know the name of my father? You will not believe it."

"Ghùl have no names." Nur spoke up from a task he was badly attempting to hide from their captive.

Amrit blinked at Esmail. "Udughul have names. Personally, I have many names. Ah, too many names. But my father was no Udughul." He growled low in his chest. "He was called Qabil. Or Cain, if it pleases you."

"So, you mean me to believe you were born of the cursed first son, and a ghùl?" Esmail spit in the dust. "That is an interesting tale, I admit. Don't believe it. But I was entertained." Esmail signaled one of the two remaining hounds to sit on Amrit's chest with his head in its slavering jaws. Then he pulled two sets of fetters from his leather bag. Reaching into the bottom of the net, he closed one set around Amrit's ankles.

"Move, and the Pshdar will bite down on that delusional skull of yours to crush it. Even if it doesn't kill you, I'm sure it won't be pleasant." He warned before lifting the net high enough over Amrit's body to bind his hands behind him. Then he nodded to Nur who moved away the hound and removed the net.

"May I sit up, please?" Amrit asked, barely keeping his excitement in check.

"Never heard a ghùl say please, either. You are truly an odd one." Esmail smirked and grabbed him from behind, forcing the bound Amrit into a kneeling position. "You may have them. I keep my promises." He dragged one ghùl body closer as Nur did the same with another.

"Thank you. Call me Amrit, please. I do not wish to be named as one of my mother's people. They irk me to no end." He inhaled the scent of death and the sour tang of the poison Nur had laced the corpses with. It was not the vomit inducing one. This one was stronger. Another he had been forced to consume lifetimes past. Grinning madly, he laughed his strange, not quite human laugh and leaned into the closest body. "Ah, I am so hungry."

Chapter 6-

Amrit awoke on the sturdy back of a mule. "It must be numb to the scent of Udughul, to not be panicking." He thought absently.

The heat of the afternoon sun beating down on him was uncomfortable but no longer unbearable. It would soon be winter. He could hear a hushed conversation just ahead of the sweating animal he was tied to. At first the words came in pieces through the fog left by the deadly nightshade he had consumed earlier in the day.

"Zale might know." Esmail spoke softly. "He's lived longer than any of us in the hunt."

"What if he's no longer there?"

"If his team has caught their prey, then they will be heading to Tyre." A pause. "There was a strange occurrence there eleven years ago that was never settled. He always goes back between jobs to try and sort it out."

Amrit laughed softly, alerting the two hunters to his awake state.

"It lives." Esmail said, stopping the mule.

Nur approached Amrit with his hand on the hilt of his sword. "Tell me, beast, what you find so amusing."

"You reminded me of something I once did in the city of Tyre." Turning his head as much as he could in his prone position, Amrit looked at the man. His eyes no longer burning pools of blood, and the madness stretched grin gone from his features. "Ah, I cannot return there for a long time now because of it. But I would readily do it again, given the opportunity. That was quite an entertaining bit of mischief."

Nur stopped when he saw their captive's eyes. "What in all of Jahan'am." He touched his forehead and heart in a warding sign. "Esmail!"

"Don't shout, I'm right here." Esmail's eyes glanced over Amrit to Nur as he signaled the Pshdars to sit. "Wait a minute." He turned back suddenly and grabbed Amrit by the hair, pulling his head back with a rough jerk.

"What happened to your eyes?" He demanded as they flashed red once more.

"I was a bit...over stimulated when we met in the morning." Amrit gasped for breath, trying to hold back the red. "Please, I will lose control." The edges of his lips were creeping upward, showing eager teeth behind them. "I do not wish to bite you."

Esmail let go of the fistful of hair, allowing Amrit's head to drop. He stepped back and watched as the creature before him tremored softly and inhaled deep breaths of air. When at last he was still, he turned brown eyes once again to look at his captors.

"Thank you." He said with a half growl before a blade drew a quicky healing line of blood from his neck.

"What sort of demon are you? I want the truth of it." Esmail's voice was low and shaking.

Amrit blinked without concern. "I gave you the truth already. I am half human, half Udughul."

"That is impossible." Nur asserted from beyond Esmail.

"Yet I am." Amrit sniffed at the air, trying to see around himself. "Ma'arra? You do not intend to parade me through the front gates like this, do you?" He fought the red induced grin trying to take over his face once again. "That would be a wonderful, terrible idea. I cannot say I recommend it."

"You talk an awful lot, demon." Esmail sighed and regarded the already visible line of refugees and merchants heading for the distant gates of Ma'arra. "I suppose I was not expecting the walled city to be so busy this time of year. How many people would you try to bite on the way through those crowded streets?" The last he asked Amrit with no real expectation of an answer, his gaze focused on the distance.

"Ah." Amrit closed his eyes, and breathing deep he gave one anyway. "Trussed up as I am? And with no thick layers of shemagh to stifle the tantalizing scent of human flesh? And with the pain of humiliation causing my self control to waver?" He clenched his jaw and maintained as neutral a tone as he could manage. "Every single one we passed. I might even gnaw off my own arm to escape the fetters you have me in."

"We should drag your sorry carcass through the streets in the camel shit. You are a plague upon this land." Nur snarled.

A half breath, inhaled quickly. Amrit was feeling the tingle of panic. And the delighted itch of his frantic hunger. "Please, please. I beg you." He whispered. "It will only end in calamity if you take me in there like this. Even the thought of it alone is too much. There is a house around the eastern side of the wall. It is small, but it is quiet and it is hidden by a garden to offer some privacy."

"Don't fall for it, Esmail." Nur glared at Amrit. "The ghùl are full of tricks and deceptions."

Amrit frowned. "Please do not call me a *ghùl*. I would gladly see my mother's people all dead and digested. And they have every justification to feel the same way about me."

"And why is that?" Esmail asked, his voice low.

"Because," Amrit took another short breath and growled low in his chest. "I am every bit the *plague* your companion called me. The Udughul have the ability to die. They have the ability to completely fill their stomachs, and not only with humans but with small rodents or insects if need be." He closed his eyes. "Ah, I hate them. I hate them, and I am filled with a burning desire to consume *them* much as my jealousy consumes *me*." He furrowed his brow, baring white teeth in a growl.

"If you need more reason to go to the house instead of through the city, the hunters you are seeking should still be in Ma'arra. The youngest at least knows of the place and has visited it. Any child in the town could send them to you if you mention the name of the owner of the house."

A kick to the side of the head made Amrit's eyes burn crimson.

"And how would you know any of this?" Nur followed up the kick with an angry punch. "The demon is full of dishonest words, Esmail. Do not fall for them."

Esmail touched his companion on the arm, his face full of sorrow and understanding. He nodded toward the gate in the distance. "I have made a decision. Go on. Find a child to send after Zale. Pay them in coin for the task, and come around to find this house surrounded by gardens." He shook his head once at Nur's unspoken protest.

"Who owns the house, demon?" Esmail turned to the monster tied to the back of the mule. "What name shall we give?"

"Ah." Amrit trembled. Then turned his head as far as he could to look at Esmail with blood red eyes. "Tell them the house of Amrit. For it is mine. I am the monster they are hunting in Ma'arra."

Esmail ran a hand over his beard, his brow creased in thought. Then he nodded once more. "Go Nur. I will meet you there."

The man spit and turned to leave, cursing under his breath and signaling one of the dogs to heel as he did.

When Nur was out of earshot, Esmail crouched down near the mule so Amrit could see him. He was amazed yet again to see his captive's eyes were no longer orbs of crimson madness.

"Do you know how we choose the ones to join us in our hunt for the ghùl?" He asked. "Traditionally, only men are trained. And we are all lone survivors of ghùl attacks. We wear our scars as badges for our trade." Lowering the neck of his shirt revealed the top of a heavy, raised line running down his chest. "Nur's entire back was torn, and he still has missing pieces of flesh in his sides. And we all lost loved ones. He hates you for it."

"*I* did not attack him." Amrit defended himself in a weak whisper. He omitted the fact that the man would not have survived him.

"True." Esmail sighed. "But do you care to tell the difference between one beetle in the dust from all the others? Especially if, as a whole, the species is given to practice harmful tendencies?" Rubbing his beard again, he let out the breath he had been holding. "How long were you in Ma'arra before Zale the hunter came for you?"

"Nearly ten years."

"That long, and you were only just recently noticed?" Esmail was genuinely surprised.

Amrit's face fell. "I do not make a practice of attacking the humans around me simply because they are there. The time I spent as a slave in the arenas left me pitifully aware of your fragile mortality. And I long ago consumed the last of the Udughul in the area. But, as I said, I cannot fill my hunger with beasts. Ah. It was a fortuitous thing when the Christian army came from the north. They do the killing. I do the eating. My conscience remains at least partially clear."

"But, I made the infelicitous mistake of eating too close to home." He gave a weak half smile. "As a result, I was seen by the older brother of a human whose company I enjoy. Ah, he will hate me once he learns what I am. And he will. Likely very soon."

A moment of silence passed between the two as they regarded each other. Finally, Esmail rocked back on his heels.

"I am beginning to think you may be closer to human than my prejudices would have me to believe." He looked around carefully. "If I unlock your ankles to allow you to sit upon the mule, so long as you do not move otherwise, I will refrain from setting my dog on you. I suppose," he grinned, "I might also try to avoid stabbing you again."

"What if I use the opportunity to kill you? I could." Amrit blinked once. "It would not be a difficult thing to accomplish even with my hands bound behind me and a hound with it's jaws locked on me."

"If so," Esmail smiled broad across his sun darkened face, "then Allah have me. But I do not think you will." He walked around the mule to Amrit's feet and paused a moment. When he spoke it sounded as though he were trying to convince himself. "You have been living in this town long enough to at least have people who know you." He set the key to the lock. "It would be shameful for me to allow them to see you degraded in such a manner."

The lock clicked and Esmail tensed, waiting for the monster to kick him, or roll off the mule, or anything. But his captive did not move. "See? You haven't attacked me. Just as I wagered." He braved.

"I do not enjoy being stabbed or mauled by hounds." Amrit chuckled low in his chest. "Even if I am guaranteed to survive, it is still an unpleasant experience. No, I will not move unless you have directed it."

"A promise from a ghùl?" Esmail was in disbelief at what he was doing. "That's new, and hardly believable."

Amrit's low laughter disappeared. "Ah, yes." He sighed. Then he spoke so quiet Esmail would have missed it, had he been any further away. "Such venomous words. Those biting barbs tearing my heart to shreds. I think I prefer the blade."

Esmail cleared his throat and helped his captive to sit upon the mule, straddling it between his knees. He then took a bedroll from a pack strapped to the mule's hind quarters. Unrolling it, he threw it around the shackles and over the top of Amrit's head.

"The wind has changed." Amrit closed his eyes and breathed in deeply, tilting his head back with care. He rumbled in his chest when he caught the scent of the humans in the distance. "It would be judicious to take a longer path around the road. Half of me may be human, but it is not always the half which governs my actions." His eyes were flashing between red and brown when he opened them again.

Esmail nodded solemnly. He signaled to the Pshdar and grabbed the rope tied to the mule. Going around the crowd would take longer than Esmail wanted, but he was certain it was the correct choice. Especially after listening to Amrit's instable arguing with himself in what sounded like multiple languages, including growls. When the one sided conversation began to become more heated, Esmail tried to redirect the monster's attention.

"So, you like to be called Amrit, yes?"

A heavy exhalation. A relieved and grateful sigh. "It is not my true name. It was given to me by a human now long dead. But it is the one I use most recently. Before you ask, you will not be able to pronounce my true name. Humans do not seem to have the capability to duplicate the complex range of sound found in the Udughul tongue. I do not think you can even hear most of it."

"I am curious, Amrit," Esmail said carefully, "if I were to ask you questions of the ghùl, would you answer them truthfully?"

Amrit pondered his answer. "So long as it would not be disastrous to do so. Some things even *I* feel are not wise to share."

"Really? Alright, then." Esmail looked at the city walls before speaking again. "You said the ghùl have names, is this true for all ghùl?"

"Yes, of course it is." Amrit's head tilted to the side. "It would be onerous to be constantly summoning each other with *hey you, no not you, the other one. No, the one chewing on a leg.*" His mouth twitched in a small, half smile. "Nothing would ever be accomplished."

"I suppose you are right." Esmail grinned. "I hear tales of a king of the ghùl. Is there any merit to them?"

Amrit's eyes grew wide and his smile became momentarily sinister. "There is. And some day, he will die to my teeth." He inhaled quickly and closed his eyes, forcing the excitement to fade. "But there is nothing more I can tell you about the ordurous, rotting bastard. Besides, you would never reach the end of the Bone Road to find him."

Swallowing hard, Esmail changed the subject. "If the ghùl have names, that would also imply that they are at least more intelligent than beasts."

"Ah, they are certainly a clever and conniving race. They have a special sort of intellect suited almost entirely for the act of deceit. And they use it well. Else they would have been wiped out by you hunters ages ago."

"Can I ask you a personal question?"

"I am the one in fetters, am I not? I am yours to interrogate as you please."

Esmail paused the mule. "How old are you, really? You can't be as young as you look, and you speak like a dottery old man."

Amrit's almost human laughter rumbled from his chest. "I suppose I do. Ah, I am too old. Other than that, I do not know for certain. Every new civilization measures time differently and I long ago gave up trying to estimate my years."

Esmail started the mule walking again. "Alright, tell me about your time as a slave. You mentioned an arena?"

"Ah, yes. I did." Amrit sighed in a way that sounded lonesome to Esmail. "Really, I was more of a captive deity. A god of death, was what they began to call me. I was traded from one reigning ruler to the next to serve entertainment through killing, or through other acts so atrocious I will not name them." He gave a sad smile. "I have always excelled at killing. They trained me in weapons, and it was at that time I learned what an unfair advantage was."

The sudden loud laugh that erupted from Amrit made Esmail jump. "Can you imagine, a child with the ability to kill with his bare hands and an inborn desire to feast on his opponents, given instruction in the sword? It was such an absurd transgression on the sanctity of life, it was lamentable! Death god, indeed." His laughter turned into that of the Udughul. "I am no god. I am an aberration."

Chapter 7-

"You have it inside?" The calm voice of Zale drifted in through the door.

They arrived hardly an hour after Esmail and Amrit, and an almost chill evening was beginning to envelope the garden.

"Ah, what a waste." Amrit had sighed as they'd passed his now wilted and vermin infested garden. "My scent has faded. I was gone too long."

Esmail had chained Amrit to the only heavy, brick support pillar in the single-room dwelling. It was a nearly barren space, with one small window set high on the northern wall to help keep out the heat. A sizable, tight sealed, clay jar in one corner held the water he used for his garden. And a couple small niches carved into the bricks were resting places for his single wooden cup, and a few other ordinary objects.

"Yes. This is a most perplexing creature." Esmail replied to the older hunter.

"You mean unnerving." Nur spit with force.

"And you are certain this is the same *Amrit* which Rayyan encountered?"

"He admitted it himself."

"It is not a *he,* Esmail. It would serve you well to remember that. Lest you fall into it's deceit." Zale's reprimand was almost kind.

"Yes, Master Zale. It claims to be half human, so I felt it might be appropriate. But I recognize your wisdom. I will keep your advice."

There was a short pause before Zale voiced his disbelief. "Half human? That doesn't even make any sense."

Amrit's heart sank when he heard Nadav speak up. "Wait, what are you talking about? *Half* human, Amrit? There is no way he is one of those monsters." His friend's scent had come in on the evening breeze, so Amrit was not unaware of the youth's presence, but the conversation was more painful to hear with his participation.

"I am going in. It can't be the same man." Nadav's uneven footsteps in the garden were stopped short.

"No, it is fine Nur. Let the boy go. It is good for him to learn the truth of things with his own eyes." Zale consented.

A moment later, Nadav half hobbled into Amrit's line of view. "Oh, Amrit!" He cried as he fell upon his friend. "It can't be true. Tell me it's all a mistake, or a bad joke."

Amrit gave a sad smile. "Look in the pocket on my right. There is something there for you."

The boy frowned and located the pocket. He was confused when he pulled out a pair of cracked, bone sand goggles.

"I promised." Amrit said looking away. "When you figured out how I never starved, I told you I would give them to you. I apologise for their state. I was not expecting the weight of a Pshdar hound to be placed upon them while stowed away.

"No." Nadav tried to push the goggles back into Amrit's pocket. "No. I've known you since I was a child, you have only been kind to me and everyone who met you. You can't be one of those vile monsters. No, I won't accept it."

Amrit closed his eyes, holding back the manic grin that was threatening his composure. "Ah, Nadav. Such harsh words." He whispered. Then only a little louder, he asked, "Do you remember the day we met?"

"Yes, it was at my parents house. They treated you like royalty that day and I had thought you must be some wandering king in disguise."

"No, Nadav, it was a good twenty days before that. You have convinced yourself it was a dream. It was not. You were kidnapped along with your twin sister, and the group was attacked by Udughul not long after they escaped beyond the city walls. I heard the screams and smelled the blood in the wind the day I was to arrive at Ma'arra. I began to kill the Udughul I found out of spite, but half of them ran from me taking you with them and leaving your twin behind."

Amrit sighed. "Ah, I was planning to help your sister before going after you, but I have always had unfortunate luck. A band of hunters had been on my trail, and one of their hounds managed to catch up to me. I had only enough time to rid myself of the dog and escape alone before I was seen. Your sister's wounds were severe, you see. I reasoned she would be better taken care of by someone who would not be tempted by the scent of her fresh spilled blood. Someone more human than I. Besides, they would have hunted me all the more zealously if they believed I had a hostage. So, I left her to be found by Zale."

"You were nearly unconscious when I found you, Nadav. The four Udughul who had run were arguing amongst themselves. A game which, in my opinion, my mother's people enjoy far too much. Should they kill you now? Or go back to kill me first, and *then* kill you? They never reached a concordance on the matter, as I had arrived to finish *them* off, instead." Keeping his eyes tightly closed, Amrit tilted his head to the side and his face slipped momentarily into the madness of his desire to consume. "Ah, they were almost satisfying to eat. I managed to find your home, when it was through. Your parents were most glad to have you returned, though they lamented the loss of your sister." Amrit breathed deep. "And from the scent on you, it seems you have been keeping company with your long lost twin while I have been away."

"That is a fine story, Amrit, but I have not been spending time with any women besides the ones in the household." Nadav scoffed.

With shut eyes, Amrit turned his head towards Rayyan, who had been standing in the doorway behind Nadav. "How do *you* remember that day, hunter?"

"Was that monstrous being truly you?" Rayyan whispered shakily. She took a half step forward and loosened her shemagh, uncovering her face and neck. The scars she bore covered her entire left cheek, running down her neck where they looked like silvery rivers across her throat.

"Hold on." Nadav fell back, fully sitting on the brick floor. "You're a woman? That's my sister?" He turned to confront Amrit and was startled by the burning color of his now open eyes. "What in Jahan'am?"

"It was. She is." Amrit offered quietly behind a creeping, crazed grin. "And with a tremendous amount of misfortune and self loathing, I am what they have named me as."

"But, but..." Nadav began, the words catching in his throat and his face distorting with revulsion.

The revelations were interrupted by the boisterous laughter of Nadav's older brother. Yahir had followed the hunters to Amrit's house. "I knew it!" He nearly shouted. "I knew I was right. You have finally caught the disgusting thing, have you? Is it dead? I would very much like to see."

The sound of him pushing his way to the door and the smell of spice preceded his gloating face. He gave Rayyan a discourteous shove with his shoulder before he spotted Amrit. "What? It's alive? Why didn't you kill the monster?"

Zale stepped in behind the loud man. "I am told it will not die. Though, I have yet to validate the claim myself."

"Then I will validate it for you." Yahir pulled a dagger from the braided belt around his waist.

Amrit's maniacal grin widened impossibly. "If *you* come close enough to touch me with that blade, I will bite off your hand." Yahir paused mid stride, his face blanching, and Amrit continued. "I have resisted consuming you for many years out of respect for your family, Yahir. Otherwise, I would surely lose no sleep over the death of one so worthless to his race."

"Then allow me." Zale drew his sword, the edge glinting in the light cast by the oil filled lantern on the low table. When the smirking demon made no move or show of protest, Zale covered the space between them and thrust the blade deep into his chest. He gave a strong twist and held the sword in place as his victim cried out in pain. He was about to remove the weapon, when he noticed odd movement beneath the torn and freshly bloodied tunic. "What dark magic is this?" He whispered. He pulled hard on his sword, extracting it and eliciting a new cry from Amrit.

"Ah." Amrit sighed as the wound healed. "It would be unwise to continue." He nearly growled, keeping his gaze away from his young friend. "I will lose control of myself, and I do not think Nadav could take much more today. The smell of his fear is nearly as thick as the look of disdain he currently bears toward me."

Yahir spit. "If the filth will not die, then drag it through the streets. Expose the monster for what it is. String it up by the well, and allow the people it has fooled to stone it until they are satisfied."

"We will not do anything tonight." Zale intervened. "It is dark now, and only dirty business is done in the night. We will decide on the fate of this ghùl when the sun shines on us."

"Fine." Yahir grunted. "But it had better be good. Or I will deal with it as I please." He left without so much as even addressing his younger brother.

"I am sorry, Nadav." Amrit offered, attempting to force himself to calm down enough for the crazed look to leave his face.

"What are we to you?" Nadav whispered. Then he snarled at Amrit, forcing the words past his teeth. "Were you only fattening us like goats? Is that why you were feeding the beggars and children? How long would you have waited until you sank your teeth into the *people* of Ma'arra?"

Amrit's heart tightened and the red left him. "Am I no longer a person, then, dear friend?" He gave a sad smile.

"I am *not* your friend!" Nadav rose to his unsteady feet. "I trusted you. I trusted you, and you used me. How many have you killed while you've been in Ma'arra? A hundred? More? You are a filthy, impure thing. And I have been stained by you."

All traces of smile left Amrit as his once friend stumbled into the night. After he could no longer hear Nadav's feet he closed his eyes and tilted his head back, ignoring Rayyan as she slipped out of the house after her long lost brother. "Ah. I can no more change the nature I was given at birth than any other creature can, dear Nadav. No matter how I try, I fear my soul will remain completely irredeemable."

With no more fortitude to mourn the loss of a cherished friendship, Amrit laughed. He laughed the low, rumbling laugh of an Udughul. He laughed the higher, smooth laugh of a human. And he laughed the desperate laugh of something not quite either.

Chapter 8 -

Esmail and Nur left with the rising dawn, taking their hounds and mule into the chill morning. Nur spat on the floor, and Esmail nodded to Amrit on their way out. Not a friendly nod. It was a resigned and obligatory acknowledgement of a night spent under his roof. They had quickly agreed that Zale might be better suited to the task of deciding how to handle the difficult conundrum of an immortal ghùl.

Zale had spent most of the night discussing the options with the other four hunters. The group had a difficult time coming upon a suitable course of action, and they all wore dark circles under their eyes as a result. Finally, it was settled that Zale and his two companions would chance taking the aberration to the holy city of Jerusalem. If nothing else, there should be some form of holy man capable of placing a blessing upon Amrit with the hope of neutralizing his immortality.

After sending Rayyan and Marin into the town to acquire a few provisions they would need for the journey south, Zale stood in the doorway and regarded Amrit in silence. He had never been so unsure when it came to one of the ghùl. There had always been a large amount of certainty in everything he knew about them.

They were cowardly. They avoided situations where they were outnumbered. They never moved alone. They could not successfully blend in with humans for any amount of time under scrutiny. They certainly weren't unable to die. It simply took more effort to kill one. Zale was finding less and less similarities between the usual ghùl he hunted, and this monster before him.

Finally, Amrit became weary of the unfocused gaze of the hunter. "It will not work." He spoke soft and subdued. "I once met the holiest of all men. I had hoped for the same solution you seek. But he renounced my petition, sending me away with little more than words to console me. And here I still am, many lifetimes later."

Zale was silent for a moment as he leaned on the doorway. He didn't trust the words of the demon. He would still drag it all the way to Jerusalem and at least attempt to follow through with the only viable idea they had been able to piece together. Even though he harbored his own misgivings concerning the outcome.

Just as he opened his mouth to say as much, the ghùl kneeling on the floor snapped it's head up. It's eyes were wide and vibrant crimson. It sniffed at the air and turned it's gaze upon Zale. "Ah, how unfortunate." A crazed grin slowly stretched it's face in madness. "Quickly, they will arrive soon. You must help me to prevent unnecessary casualties."

Zale frowned. "What deception are you trying to convince me of?"

"It seems as though a mob has been formed. You will hear them soon, their raised voices are filled with vindication." The word *Alghul* rang through the morning air in painful volleys, wrenching at Amrit's heart. "I can already feel the pull of my desire to consume. Please, look to the niche in the wall behind me. Next to the cup, there is an iron rod with a hole at either end. Run a rope or leather thong through the holes and strap it tightly in my teeth."

"Why, ghúl? So I will be close enough to bite?" Zale crossed his arms over his chest.

"Ah, please." Amrit tilted his head back, the panic was threatening to overcome him. "If you do not, many will suffer needlessly. And I will dine."

Zale narrowed his eyes at his captive then turned to look outside. He had finally heard the distant sound of many people. And the noise was growing closer. "Fine." He said. "Bite me, and I shall remove your head."

Pulling a cord from the pouch at his waist, Zale strode across the small abode and set to the task requested of him. All the while keeping his eyes on the unmoving ghúl in case it decided to snap at him.

When the job was done, he stepped back and watched as the ghùl's shoulders relaxed. It nodded what could be assumed to be a thank you before Zale walked to the garden to intercept the group headed their way.

Amrit closed his eyes and breathed deep in an attempt to regain his quavering self control. He growled low in his throat when the sound of the mob reached his sensitive ears. He could hear them trampling what was left of the vegetation. The crack of snapping branches was followed by the smell of burning as they used his trees to light as makeshift torches.

When Nadav's voice carried through the ruckus, Amrit nearly laughed for the tragedy of it. He bit down on the iron between his teeth hard enough to taste his own blood.

"Don't stand in the way, hunter." Nadav addressed Zale resolutely. "How many people has it killed already? How many more will you let it have because of your ineptitude?"

"If *you* can't kill it, let us take it." Yahir added, supporting his younger brother. "Or we will burn the house down with it inside, and you alongside it if we must."

"While I understand the feeling of betrayal and resentment you are likely experiencing, this is not the answer." Zale reproached the siblings calmly. "Though, I suppose it would be pointless of me to attempt to change your minds at this point. Where are my colleagues? Did you delay them in town so they could not rush back to warn me?"

"They are safe," Yahir's voice, "for now. Give us the demon and they will be even safer still."

A heavy sigh, followed by what could have been Zale's hands dropping to his sides. "I will not stand in your way. But at this point, I relinquish all responsibility. I will gather my colleagues and we will leave Ma'arra."

Yahir came into Amrit's view, his face betraying the sadistic pleasure he was feeling. He pulled his short knife from the braided belt at his waist and advanced on Amrit's kneeling form.

"Hello again, demon." He huffed with a superior tone. "I see your threat to bite my hand off is no longer an issue."

"Just get it done, Yahir. The faster you cut the rope, the faster we will be finished here." Amrit looked Nadav in the eyes without wavering as the youth spoke.

Nadav spat on his one time friend. "Do not look at me, monster. Your filthy gaze will only dirty me further."

Others streamed in around Nadav and began to help Yahir. "It's true, then." One said. "Just look at those eyes!" They cut the rope that had been tied through his fetters and dragged him across the floor by his still bound hands, kicking and hitting him as they did. They did not hold back their tongues, either. Throwing insults at him the whole time. Amrit growled curses at his assailants, the madness in his eyes growing deeper with every passing moment.

A rope was looped over Amrit's head and tightened around his neck. While he struggled for breath, they attached the other end of his noose to a horse. It was difficult work, with the horse panicking over the scent of the Alghul so near. But they managed it, and a lean man took the reigns and climbed atop the animal.

Nadav leaned in and looked at Amrit, glaring straight into his crazed, red eyes. "You will regret the last ten years, demon. If I had known from the start, I would never have kept your company." He stood and signaled the rider.

The man kicked the horse in the flank and the crowd parted to make way.

Amrit was dragged all along the path, then through the gates. The horse did not slow, though, and kept pulling him through the dusty streets of Ma'arra. Pedestrians were forced to the side in their wake, many becoming excited at the prospect of a public display. Amrit felt the short lived sting of wounds on his body as though they were far away. The wrenching of his heart easily overshadowed every other pain.

The horse was pulled up by the well and Amrit tumbled to a stop behind it. He had no chance to catch his breath or take stock of his surroundings, however. More men had been waiting for their arrival. One grabbed him by the hair, and another by his fetters, digging them into his wrists. All the while insulting and spitting on Amrit.

He was dragged to an archway leading down a side path, which had been overthrown with a rope. The rope was secured around his fetters, and the slack was pulled from the rope until Amrit felt his arms drawn up behind him. He was raised off the ground in slow, painful jerks until his feet no longer touched the ground and all his weight was suspended on his arms and shoulders behind him.

The growing crowd kept some distance between the red eyed monster and themselves. Women with children gripped their tiny hands fiercely, as though the demon would eat them otherwise. Men muttered and gestured towards Amrit with excitement and righteous indignation. Amrit's heart burned with the hatred he saw on their faces. The open displays of disgust and contempt made him seethe with his own anger.

Ten years. Ten years he had lived near these people. Had helped them in every way he could, in any way they needed. Spoken with them. Called some of them friend. All without allowing his hunger to overtake him. All without harming a single decent citizen. He had even rid the city of some of the most dangerous humans hiding in the shadows. The murderers and rapists. In fact, no longer did people worry about the Udughul when wandering outside the gates, thanks to his efforts.

But all they saw now, was the color of his eyes. The vibrant blood red. The distinguishing mark of his mother's people. The eyes of a monster.

Amrit's arms had gone numb by the time Nadav caught up to the crowd. His young features were distorted with an unbridled resentment and rage. He was the first to cast a stone, hitting Amrit in the chest.

"You disgusting miscreation!" He threw another, causing a gash on Amrit's madly grinning jawline below the metal in his mouth.

The crowd gasped and renewed it's chittering when the wound closed as they watched. "Truly a demon!" They cried. "Kill it!" They shouted. "Allah save us." They pleaded.

A rain of stones and refuse stormed against him, cutting and bruising him. But he hardly noticed the stinging. He paid no mind to the dull aches. The pain of the lacerations to his fragile heart anxiously swallowed everything else as he stared at Nadav with eager, madness filled eyes.

Nadav faltered under the unblinking gaze of the monster. He blanched and pushed his way through the crowd, leaving Amrit to the torture he had devised. And Amrit rumbled a sad chuckle as he watched the youth walk away.

Chapter 9

The crowd did not let up until the day had ended and it was too dark to see anything but Amrit's eerie glowing eyes. Yahir and Seff had even made an appearance during the day. Yahir vaunting his pride at discovering the unholy creature, while Seff wrung his hands nervously in the presence of the Alghul. Even one restrained as Amrit was, seemed to be too much for the anxious man.

A guard was set nearby through the night. But he maintained a distance, occasionally glancing to Amrit, and quickly turning away from the unwavering, crimson stare.

The crowd returned early the next morning, obviously unsatisfied with the violence of the previous day. Here was a victim they could punish endlessly. One that they could abuse without the fear of it's death weighing on them. It was only a soulless monster, after all.

Amrit lost track of the days. They melted together in a haze of consistent torture and emotional suffering as it became more chill and overcast with winter. At first, he held onto the spectral fragment of his sanity. He had grasped at the fading clarity of thought. A rapidly drying oasis caught in the middle of a drought.

But something snapped in him when the children started to emulate their parents, hurling insults and animal feces. All he could see now was red. All he felt was betrayed, and hungry. The only thing occupying his mind was his desire to devour. His desire to kill. To bite. To eat. To consume. To destroy. To feel the last quivering spasms of fresh meat in his teeth.

He hardly noticed when the humans began to behave differently. Whispering to each other in huddled groups. Nervously bragging about the strength of the walls. He barely registered the noise coming from outside the city. The smell of smoke on the wind. The heavy feeling of disquiet.

Then, Amrit was surprised one day when the sun rose and no one came to torture him. He raised his head to look around, and saw he had no guard. In fact, the square was empty. He spent the day alone, with only the scent of fire and early winter. The solitude was a welcome reprieve and he regained a fraction of his sanity. Enough to finally notice that something was terribly wrong in the city of Ma'arra.

When night had fallen in earnest, he had calmed enough for the red to leave him. He tilted his head curiously when he saw shadows against the stars, moving along the top of the closest portion of the city wall. He sniffed the air and sneezed when he inhaled a nose full of Ras El Hanout, the mix of spice that the hunters used to deter the Udughul.

Amrit growled softly around the iron between his teeth as Rayyan stepped into the square.

"Ghùl." She whispered. "Is your mind clear?"

Being unable to give a verbal answer she would understand, Amrit nodded his head in the dark, hoping she could see.

"I came back for Nadav. But I had to sneak in, and I left my Pshdars in what remains of your garden. I don't know if you can tell from here, the Christian army has returned and they're laying siege on Ma'arra. I think they will attempt to breach the walls tonight."

"I am going to remove the metal from your mouth." She continued. "You bite me, and I will leave you here to be gutted by the Christians."

When Amrit made no indication that he would move, she stepped in cautiously and used a slender knife to slit the cord from behind his head.

Amrit let the iron fall to the ground with a dull thud in the dust. He stretched his jaw and sighed in relief. "Thank you." He said in his quiet way. Then he tilted his head at the hunter. "Why are you here, instead of with Nadav?"

"I need your help." She stepped back just a little. "The estate was empty. I can't find Nadav or the rest of the family. I couldn't even locate the servants. I assume you are able to follow scents the way other ghùl do?"

"I am." Amrit's chest tightened when he thought of playing with the human children only months before, locating each of them by scent alone.

"I have little trust in you, but you were good to me, and you were good to the people of this town for ten years. I don't think you would turn on them so easily." Rayyan looked at Amrit in the dark, the uncertainty on her face as clear to him as if the sun yet shone.

"I am finished with humans." Amrit assured her with as little emotion as he could manage. "I have suffered the betrayal of those close to me enough to fill the sea. If you release me, I will leave this place. And I do not think I shall return."

He closed his eyes then, and sighed. A pained look on his pale face. "Yet, I suppose that, despite the change of heart Nadav has had concerning our friendship, I would never forgive myself if I simply left him here to fend against an army alone." When he opened his eyes to look at Rayyan, they were flickering red in the darkness as he strained to push down his tumultuous emotions. "I will help you to find Nadav and the rest of your family. I will do my best to see you escape Ma'arra, and then you will never see me again."

Rayyan let out the breath she had been holding. "Thank you." She whispered and hurried to the knot tied in the rope which held Amrit aloft. After some struggling behind him, she admitted defeat. "It has been pulled taut for too long, I can't untie it."

The sound of her drawing the slender knife came before she spoke again. "Sorry for this." She cut the rope in three rough strokes.

Amrit fell, striking the ground with legs numb from dangling so long. He rolled to his stomach and allowed the feeling to return to his fingers, then his hands and arms as he breathed in the cold dust. He held as still as death as Rayyan undid the puzzle lock on his fetters, releasing his arms and legs.

"Thank you." Amrit said before he rose to his feet in a slow, predatory manner. "The wall has already been breached. They were climbing over as you arrived." With eyes continuing to flash back and forth between sanity and the flooding of blood red, he led Rayyan into the shadowed streets towards the house of Nadav's family.

They took longer than Amrit would have liked. He had to shove the hunter into deep shadows numerous times to avoid detection by the Christians. And to avoid the small skirmishes that broke out whenever the invading knights were challenged. When they finally reached their destination, he was becoming irritable with the tension of remaining alert for yet apart from the enticing violence.

They entered the estate from the back to avoid being seen. Amrit breathed deep, closing his eyes and tilting his head to the side. "They left at least a day ago. Though, the servants were here most likely until just before you arrived." He walked through the empty house, breathing in the scents of all the missing inhabitants, in case Rayyan had overlooked something during her original visit to the house. Upon exiting the building neither were surprised to find the fighting had grown louder.

"The gates must have been opened." Rayyan offered in a whisper.

Amrit nodded in agreement, while clenching his jaw in a delirious grin. "Then it seems we have even more need to make haste. I am ashamed to admit that I tend to have difficulty maintaining my self control around bloodshed." He noted the look of worry on Rayyan's moonlit face. "Though, I believe I will be able to make it. If we manage to avoid any direct confrontation, I can make it."

The pale man led the way through the back streets, and between houses and buildings which were nearly stacked on top of each other in the older parts of town. He paused at each intersection to sniff at the air, or the walls and ground, much the way the Pshdars would have done, had Rayyan been able to get them into Ma'arra unnoticed by the Christians.

Amrit stopped a short way from a minor mosque, his restless insanity barely restrained in his pale features. The fighting had become cacophonous in the night as the city guards uselessly attempted to quell the insurgent army. All the while, Amrit was struggling to subdue his own inner conflict.

"They are in the mosque." Amrit said between impatient teeth. "I do not know whether you are able to see it in the dark, but it looks as though the windows and doors to the lower levels have been sealed. I can get you to the upper windows, if you are willing to trust an Udughul to carry you there."

Rayyan looked across the intersection between them and towards the building in question. She could see none of that in the dark. She frowned before nodding.

"Climb on." Amrit turned around and pointed a thumb at his back. After only a brief hesitation, the hunter did as she was bade. A low growl emitted from Amrit's chest as she wrapped her arms and legs around him and he shuddered with the effort of controlling himself. "Please make sure you do not move too much. Remember that I am already struggling against my nature with your closeness. I have a strong desire to avoid waking from my usual delirium to discover that I am biting you."

Rayyan swallowed the lump that had formed in her throat and Amrit took off along the shadows lining the intersection. When it seemed as though he would have to leave the relative obscurity the buildings offered, he leapt off the ground and went bounding up between walls to the rooftop across the street from the mosque.

"I am going to jump." He warned. "Be prepared for the landing, it may be rough."

Then he sped across the flat rooftop, and pushed off the edge to fly over the street. His fingers and bare feet found scarcely enough purchase in the stone as he caught himself. He clenched his teeth to avoid snapping at the arm of the woman clinging frantically to his back. Her grip had tightened with fear, and Amrit tapped her elbow to remind her that he still needed to be able breathe at least a little in order to maintain his sanity.

Rayyan was amazed at his strength, the way he scaled the nearly smooth wall to the only open window on their side of the building was fascinating. Especially while carrying her on his back as he was. She had seen the strength of the ghùl when fighting them, but she'd never witnessed it being used in such a way.

Amrit gripped onto the ledge of the open window and paused, listening to the interior for occupants. When he was satisfied that it was an empty room, he helped the hunter to scramble through first. He glanced down at the street and watched as a mass of Christian soldiers smashed in doors a short distance from the mosque. "We must leave quickly. They will soon be here." Amrit insisted as he entered the window.

He hesitated at the exit to the small space. "Ah, it might be best if I wait here." His glowing, red eyes wide with excitement. "I do not believe any of the people downstairs will be glad to see me. Least of all in my current unstable state."

Rayyan agreed solemnly, and left him behind in the dark.

From the high window, he watched the mob draw ever closer to the mosque. The sound of death and the rich scent of blood strengthening with each passing moment. He growled quiet arguments with himself as he hid in the shadows for what felt like a tiny eternity. He could kill a few and return oh, so quickly. It would be easy. It would be gratifying. Satisfying. Delightful. Delicious.

When Amrit finally heard the hunter returning, there were only two sets of footsteps ascending to his hiding place. Nadav's scent floated through the doorway before him and Amrit's heart clenched with the fresh memory of the pain caused by his once dear friend.

"None of the others would come. They are clinging to the hope that the Christians will keep their word and spare them." Rayyan announced in a whisper, and Nadav avoided Amrit's deranged gaze. "What little good it will do them."

"I pray their hopes are not unfounded." Amrit tilted his head to the side. "I rather like your family, and I wish them no ill fortune."

Nadav sneered and huffed his disbelief.

They were interrupted by a banging on the front door that was loud enough to carry up the stairs. Amrit hung precariously out the window to see, as Rayyan sped back down the stairs. Shouting preempted the unbarring of the door as Amrit watched with deranged excitement, his face already stretched in the desirous pull of fervid madness.

"They will all die. The Christian army will kill them all." Amrit's head weaved as if drunk as he pulled himself back inside.

"No," Nadav argued. "They were offering our safety if we surrender! Didn't you hear them?"

Amrit closed his eyes and breathed in as deep as he could. "I can smell the blood on them, dear Nadav. I have been listening to them speak to one another in their own tongues. They are zealous, and they are desperate."

When he snapped his eyes open to look directly at Nadav, Amrit tilted his head to the side and asked, "Do you wish for me to intervene? It may still go badly, if I do. Though, it will be for a different reason altogether."

Nadav swallowed, and just as he opened his mouth to reply, the first piercing scream resounded in the darkness. "Yes!" He shouted and Amrit was surging out the window before he finished the word. The eerie sound of his inhuman laughter echoing in the dark emptiness he left behind him.

Chapter 10

A blur of burning red orbs gleamed in the torchlight accompanied by the white of teeth presenting themselves giddily through voracious grinning lips. Some of the soldiers were already inside, and none saw Amrit's rapid descent from above. Landing on top of one of the invading men, Amrit broke his neck then picked up the discarded sword as the others who had yet to enter the mosque stepped back in surprise.

Uncertainty and fear undulated through the men and Amrit grinned wide and wild at them. "You are most fortunate." He said in one of their languages. "The good people you are killing are already afraid of me, you see. So, you will die by the sword, as soldiers. Instead of being eaten alive, like you deserve, as the common criminals you are. It is a shame, though, since I am so very hungry."

Amrit gave the men no time to reply as he began to skilfully slice into his opponents with the appropriated blade. The first to fall spilled his intestines on the street before he could even raise his own weapon. The second had his hamstrings severed and he cried out with the pain. After a third was literally disarmed, the rest of the group made as if to run, but Amrit was on them with inhuman speed. None of them made it far from the mosque. When the last was killed he turned his blood splattered face skyward and greedily inhaled the scent of death, before heading inside.

He crossed the threshold to the sacred building and was glad to find that the few soldiers who had entered were now dead. Unfortunately, they had taken at least ten with them. Nadav's sister and father were among the number, and Amrit silently mourned their loss. The wailing of Nadav's now orphaned niece was loud against his blood induced high.

"Alghul! It's the demon!" Someone shouted, drawing Amrit's burning stare and alerting the others to his quiet presence.

The few who had been able to acquire swords during the short fight placed themselves between the monster in the doorway and the other humans, their hands shaking with uncertainty. Amrit tilted his head to the side and bit his teeth together until he tasted his own blood. "I have no desire to harm any of you."

He spoke softly through his delirious smile. "However, if you continue to point your swords at me, I may not be able to restrain myself for very much longer."

Rayyan pushed her way through the quaking ring of defenders, a gash on her arm bleeding through her ruined sleeve. Her shemagh undone, and hanging loose. "Move, damn it!" She nearly shouted, Nadav following in her wake.

"More are on the way." Amrit shivered with barely repressed excitement. He was already losing himself to the pull of his hunger. "We have to go. Now."

"We have to collect my mother, we can't leave her here like this. And we don't know where Yahir is." Nadav's face was pale but his voice remained steady despite the sorrow he was feeling.

"Nadav, you are going with that demon?" The rug weaver, a man called Hassan, sneered in disgust. "We should kill it, then turn to killing the bastards who did *this*!" He waved a hand toward Nadav's mother, who was weeping loudly over the bodies of her husband and daughter while cradling the screaming infant. "I think they are here because of that *monster* in the first place. We're being punished for harboring the spawn of Jahan'am for so long!"

Many nodded and muttered in agreement with the accusation. They had never had such a problem before. Never had an army from the north come specifically to take the holy lands by force. Never had so many of their neighboring towns been routed so thoroughly. Never had the walls of Ma'arra been breached.

Not before the desert demon joined them.

Amrit growled through his mad grin, but he did not move. He worried the already volatile and frightened humans would decide to attack him if he even dared to breathe. So, he stood as still as death in the doorway, attempting to keep himself from killing them all.

"That's shit, and you know it." Rayyan placed herself between Amrit and the others. "All I have heard of Amrit is good. He saved Nadav when he was kidnapped as a child. Brought him back from a death in the desert. He fed your starving people with the crops he labored alone to grow, despite having no use for any of them himself. He repaired walls and doorways of houses and carried water for the elderly and infirm. He always treated your children kindly and with gentleness."

She glanced back at the man she was defending and swallowed the lump in her throat. "Ghùl, he may be. But he is no more a monster than any of you."

Hassan pointed at Rayyan. "Look at that ruined face, she's likely a demon as well, and she's only spreading distraction." He accused her with venomous enmity. "It's best we kill them both and be done with this wretched curse!" He lunged at Rayyan, his newly acquired sword held out to stab her in the heart.

Amrit seized the hunter by the elbow and swung her around, putting his own back before the offending blade. He grit teeth against the expected sting of metal piercing his flesh. But it did not come. Instead he heard the heartbreaking squelch of muscle torn open. He smelled the iron rich scent of fresh spilled blood. He felt a warm body fall against his own, before sliding to the floor.

He already knew before he twisted around. He knew before he settled tear stung eyes on the rapidly cooling corpse lying in a growing stain of crimson. He knew before the heart shattering cry of the female hunter he had protected reached his ears, that Nadav was dead.

Amrit felt the world slow around him. He felt the weight of his emotions swirl together until they were all one color in his void. He took in one long, and shaking breath, then stilled. His focus gone, the anchor to his lucidity shattered.

He was a blur of anger and wild joy as he sprung over the body at his feet. Amrit knocked the sword from Hassan's grip with the back of his left hand. And grabbing the man by the face with his right hand, he pushed him over backwards, smashing his head into the floor in one smooth and practiced motion.

Amrit growled happily in his chest while licking the blood and grey matter from his fingers.

It took only a second for the panic to set in, once the humans realized what had happened. The renewed screaming and the smell of fear was intoxicating to the pale monster in their midst. He laughed as he bit into soft throats. He smirked as he broke limbs. He cavorted and danced in the carnage. All the while sinking ever deeper into the flood of crimson that had overtaken him. He no longer recognized any of the faces. They were only a meal, now.

Following the humans as they fled the mosque, he carried his carnage into the streets of Ma'arra, spreading the panic ever wider around him. He killed without hesitation as he came upon new victims. He killed indiscriminately. Christian and Muslim. Male and female. Old and young. Hostile and harmless. What little humanity Amrit had been safeguarding inside of him, had been swallowed up by the madness when Nadav died.

The sun was casting a soft pink haze over the city walls when Amrit finally stopped killing. He stood by the well in the center of town without moving. His head turned to the rising dawn. Tears leaving paths in the drying blood smeared over his face. The mad smile had gone, leaving only sorrow behind.

He smelled spice and turned to look at the approaching hunter with clear, brown eyes. She was holding her infant niece, who was sleeping in her arms.

"Amrit." She spoke softly, her gaze taking in the remnants of Amrit's frenzied consumption.

"I am leaving now. I have no ties left here. They have all perished."

Amrit screwed up his face in frustration. "Was it me, who killed your mother?"

Shaking her head, she answered. "No. She took her own life after handing the babe over to me."

Turning to walk away, Amrit motioned for Rayyan to follow. He took her through the ghostly quiet streets and she tried to avoid looking too hard at any of the ruined corpses. Instead of going to one of the gates, Amrit scooped her up in his arms and found his way to a rooftop, where he jumped to the wall with ease. "Hold the infant close." He warned before dropping silently to the ground on the other side. Rayyan's shaking legs made it difficult for her to stand after he set her gently down.

They walked without speaking the entire way to the burned down ruins of Amrit's house and garden. He growled his sorrow in his throat, as they neared the tumbled stone border. But he stopped in the road, since he could smell the hunter's two Pshdar hounds. And he knew they would soon smell him as well.

"Amrit." Rayyan sighed. "If it means anything at all, I am truly sorry. I wish I had been able to do something for Nadav." She turned her scarred face towards the town. "I am ashamed, but a part of me agreed with the idea that this happened because you were here. Only Allah knows for certain, though. Right?"

"It is regrettable," Amrit replied, "but I have long known that my soul is irredeemable. No amount of charity or repentance will change it. I will not spare you or your companions if we meet again. Goodbye, Rayyan."

A tear streaked down the woman's cheek as she stood looking at the smoke rising above the walls of Ma'arra. Her hounds began to bray from the opposite side of the garden and she knew that Amrit was gone. She did not even have to turn around to verify his absence. Holding the infant close, she fell to her knees in the dust of the path and wept for the loss of a family she had only just found. She wept for the orphaned child in her arms.

She wept for Ma'arra. She wept for Amrit.

Back inside the city, Amrit watched as the victorious invaders failed to discover any of the riches or stores of food they had been promised upon the success of their drawn out siege. They were ghosts of their former strength. They were a broken and forlorn army.

"Ah." Amrit grinned viciously to himself. "They were kind enough to provide substance for me. I should be gracious and offer my assistance in the same manner."

Approaching a group of eleven exhausted men, Amrit addressed them in the language he had heard them speaking to each other. "Why do you stand there grumbling about your shrinking stomachs? Yes, the larders may be empty." He smiled his most charming smile and swept his hand in a wide arc over the carnage left from the night. "But it seems to me that there is plenty of meat to go around."

Later, when the Christians returned home, and when they spoke of that unholy day in disgraced whispers, they wept while remembering the wonderful smell of woeful, heinous meat cooking over fires. They shuddered to recall the unsettling sound of inhuman laughter carried on the wind as they abandoned their humanity in the walled city of Marre.

Made in the USA
Coppell, TX
18 August 2021